A FAMILY APART 5.4

Frances felt herself drawn to look at the people in the room, fearfully searching one face, then another, for hopeful signs. Round or long, wrinkled or plumply red-cheeked, bushy-eyebrowed or scruffily bearded, no matter; every pair of eyes in every face stared intently at the children. Frances couldn't tell what they were thinking. She tried to look away, but couldn't. For a moment she felt dizzy, and her stomach churned. Desperately, she held Petey even more tightly. Who were all these strangers? Would any of them choose the Kelly children to be their own? What if no one wanted them? What would happen to them then?

A Family Apart

Joan Lowery Nixon

BANTAM BOOKS
NEW YORK · TORONTO · LONDON · SYDNEY · AUCKLAND

RL 6, IL age 10 and up

A FAMILY APART

A Bantam Book
Bantam hardcover edition / October 1987
Bantam paperback edition / December 1988

ISBN 0-553-27478-3

Published simultaneously in the United States and Canada

PRINTED IN THE UNITED STATES OF AMERICA

OPM   15 14 13 12 11 10 9 8

To my friend
Dan Weiss

A Note From the Author

During the years from 1854 to 1929, the Children's Aid Society, founded by Charles Loring Brace, sent more than 100,000 children on orphan trains from the slums of New York City to new homes in the West. This placing-out program was so successful that other groups, such as the New York Foundling Hospital, followed the example.

The Orphan Train Quartet was inspired by the true stories of these children; but the characters in the series, their adventures, and the dates of their arrival are entirely fictional. We chose St. Joseph, Missouri, between the years 1860 and 1880 as our setting in order to place our characters in one of the most exciting periods of American history. As for the historical figures who enter these stories—they very well could have been at the places described at the proper times to touch the lives of the children who came west on the orphan trains.

Joan Lowery Nixon

A Family Apart

1

JENNIFER SHOOK BACK her long, dark hair, damp from the summer's heat. "I wish we were home," she snapped so suddenly that she startled her younger brother Jeff, who was sitting on the steps of the front porch. "It's so boring. I miss the city. I miss my friends. I wish, oh, how I wish, we were home."

"Stop wishing," Jeff grumbled. "We haven't got a home." He squinted and slowly aimed, preparing to throw a pebble along the gravel path that led from the front porch of Grandma Briley's house to the road.

Just as he let it fly, Jennifer deliberately nudged his shoulder, causing the pebble to flop onto the grass.

"Hey!" Jeff shouted. "Cut that out!"

"Then don't say dumb stuff like that. We do too have a home. At least we will when Dad gets through with his assignment overseas."

"You know what I mean," Jeff said. He quickly

aimed and threw another pebble before Jennifer could interfere.

"I miss Dad," Jennifer said.

"I miss Mom, too," Jeff said.

"Mom? How can you miss Mom? She's right here."

"No, she's not. She's upstairs working away on that novel that never seems to get finished."

"That's not her fault. She keeps getting interrupted. Anyhow, that was the whole point of our spending the summer here in Missouri, so Mom could concentrate on her writing and we could get to know Grandma better."

"Grandma's almost as busy as Mom," Jeff complained. "In the morning she's jogging, in the afternoon she's working for that historical society, and at night she goes to City Council meetings."

Jennifer nodded. "And here we are stuck out in the middle of no place with nothing to do."

She heard a chuckle behind them, then a click as the screen door opened. " 'Out in the middle of no place'?" Grandma said as she squeezed onto the top step between them. "Well, I'll grant that northwest Missouri doesn't have all the excitement to offer that Washington, D.C., has, but you could hardly call it 'no place.' "

Jennifer felt her face grow even warmer. She pushed at the hair that clung damply to her cheeks and stammered, "I didn't mean—uh—that is—it's different in Missouri, and—"

Grandma tilted her head and studied Jennifer. "You know, you'd be a lot cooler with that lovely long hair off your neck." She got up, tugging down her shorts, and held out a hand to help Jennifer up. "Come with me— both of you. I've got something to show you that ought to relieve your boredom."

As soon as they reached their grandmother's bedroom, she pointed to the bed. "First, we'll take care of that long hair," she said. "Have a seat, Jennifer. Just give me one minute, and you'll see what I mean."

Jennifer stared at Grandma's own short-cropped curls and opened her mouth to protest. "You're not going to—" she began, but she relaxed with a grateful sigh when Grandma simply picked up a silver-backed hairbrush. The rhythmic strokes of the brush were soothing, and soon Jennifer's hair was swirled over her grandmother's left hand.

"Jeff," Grandma said, "will you please hand me a few bobby pins from that box on my dresser? There ought to still be a few of them in there."

"Bobby pins!" Jennifer gasped. Nobody used bobby pins! What in the world was she going to look like?

Her grandmother poked and patted at Jennifer's hair. Finally she said, "Stand up and look in the mirror, Jennifer. My, I've got a beautiful granddaughter."

Jennifer stared at the face in the wood-framed mirror that hung over Grandma's dresser. Her hair was parted in the middle and caught in a bun low on her neck. She looked older than fifteen. It wasn't so bad—kind of old-fashioned, but actually pretty nice. Lightly touching her hair, she sneaked another look, then met her grandmother's friendly grin. "Thanks," Jennifer said.

"Now," Grandma said, "wait till you see this." She bent to reach into the low cedar chest that stood in the corner of the room and took out a book covered with faded blue fabric. She opened it carefully and removed a sepia-toned photograph. Without a word she handed the photograph to Jennifer.

Jennifer felt prickles dart up her backbone as her eyes met those of the slender, dark-haired girl in the photograph. "Who is this girl?" Jennifer asked. "She looks like me."

"The young woman was my grandmother's mother," Grandma explained, "and when she was your age her name was Frances Mary Kelly."

Jennifer studied the photograph. "How old is she here?"

"About eighteen, I would guess."

"Do you know anything about her?"

"When Frances was thirteen years old—about your age, Jeff—she was an Orphan Train child, sent from New York City to St. Joseph, Missouri," Grandma said. "That was in 1860, just before the beginning of the Civil War."

Jeff took another look at the photograph. "What's an Orphan Train child?"

"I believe I'll let Frances Mary tell you," his grandmother said. She held out the book to Jeff. "Frances Mary wrote about her own life and the lives of her brothers and sisters and friends. If you think Missouri is a dull place, wait until you hear these stories. They're full of bandits and runaways and battles and all sorts of excitement. Why, one time Frances was almost arrested!"

Jeff eagerly opened the book, allowing Jennifer to bend close to him.

"It's too hard to read this," he finally said. "The writing looks like little spider tracks."

"And in places the ink's faded." Jennifer peered intently, surprised at her disappointment. "I can't read it, either."

"Never mind," Grandma said. "I've read these stories over and over, and I'll be glad to tell them to you. Let's find a comfortable place on the screened porch where the breeze will cool us, and I'll tell you about Frances Mary Kelly, your own great-great-great-grandmother."

Jennifer and Jeff followed their grandmother to the

shaded, breezy room with the wide-open windows. Jeff plopped on the floor, and Jennifer—remembering the graceful girl in the photograph—sank slowly into a plump-cushioned wicker chair.

"Even this journal has a story in itself," Grandma said, "so I'll read some of Frances Mary's own words."

Early this morning, as the sun rose on the anniversary of my birthdate, my dearest love gifted me with two silver-edged combs and this book, bound in blue.

He gently took the hairbrush from my hand and wound my dark hair around his fingers. "The combs are to capture this silken hair of yours, Frances Mary," he said, "and the journal is to capture all the stories you carry in your heart."

"But I've told you the stories," I said.

"You've told me, yes. But there will be others who will want to hear them."

I held the book on my lap, sliding the tips of my fingers over its soft, smooth cover. "I'm not sure where to begin."

"Begin with your family," he said. "Begin when you were very young in New York. Begin with your own story."

2

FRANCES MARY KELLY ran into the cobbled street, carefully dodging between two polished and shining hansom cabs. Hurry! She had to hurry. Mr. Lomax, who managed the office building where Frances and Ma worked as scrubwomen, had given her an errand and told her to run. Usually he didn't complain; but the last time, after he'd sent her to pick up a package, he had grumbled that she had dawdled and had docked ten cents from her weekly pay. She was terrified that he'd do it again. The family needed every penny.

Late September's warm weather had been swept away by a sudden chill wind from the north. Frances tightly clutched her thin, black shawl in one hand and the envelope Mr. Lomax had given her in the other. She darted forward across Fifth Avenue just as the huge, rumbling, iron-rimmed wheel of a cab dropped into a rut in the street in front of her, drenching the skirt of her faded brown dress and her bare feet with cold, muddy water. She jumped backward, crying out.

"Watch where you're goin'!" The driver leaned from his high perch at the back of the cab, yelling and brandishing his whip.

Shivering, her wet legs aching from the cold, Frances scrambled onto the sidewalk. Two more blocks to go. Fighting back tears, she ran down the sidewalk, ducking in and out among the pedestrians, until she came to her destination, a dark brick building with ornate cornices over the doors and windows. Frances shoved open the heavy paneled door and, after checking the names on the inner doors, found the right one and knocked.

"Come in," a deep voice called.

She pushed open the door and peered into a large, cluttered room. One wall was lined with bookshelves that were filled with dusty books bound in red, brown, and black leather. Frances gasped to see them all. Oh! If only she had so many books to read!

"What do you want?"

She whirled to face a bald, round gentleman who sat in a tall chair behind a desk that needed a good cleaning. An inkstand balanced precariously on top of a stack of scattered papers; and a greasy china plate, which held a dried crust of bread and a scattering of cheese crumbs, topped a stack of long, green, leather-bound books. Frances closed her eyes, inhaling the cheese's pungent odor. She'd had potatoes, cabbage, and the sausage her brother Mike had brought home at noon, but her stomach rumbled hungrily. There wasn't ever quite enough food to stop that.

The carpet was warm, and she curled and uncurled her bare toes against it. Ma was putting aside as much as she could to buy shoes for everyone for the winter, but the cold had come early this year, and there wasn't enough money for shoes yet.

"Speak up!" the man ordered.

Frances's eyes flew open in fright. What would happen to her job if the gentleman told Mr. Lomax that he'd been obliged to speak to her twice? "I'm sorry, sir. Are you Mr. Waterfield?"

"Of course I am," he muttered. "What business do you have with me?"

Resentful that she had no choice but to be polite to this horrible, greasy-lipped person, she thrust the envelope toward him, and he half rose from his chair to snatch it. His vest strained to stay fastened over his stomach, and one of the buttons had popped.

To keep herself from staring, Frances looked down at the floor. A crumpled newspaper lay near her toes. She picked it up and skimmed the headlines: "Discussion of treaty with China" ... "*Lady Elgin* Sunk!!! 400 Lives Lost!!!" ... "From Missouri: Mr. S. Harbaugh, Lexington newspaper publisher, was run out of town by fifteen proslavery men and his printing office destroyed."

An advertisement offered, "*The Life of Abraham Lincoln* by an Illinois Republican who knows well the man and his history ... a compact pamphlet ... 4 cents a copy ... address the *Tribune*, Tribune Building, New York." Abraham Lincoln was running for president of the United States, and the voting would be the next month. Da had admired the man and had told her about him. How she would love to read that pamphlet!

Frances blurted out, "Sir, if you no longer want this newspaper, may I have it?"

Mr. Waterfield raised his head from the letter he was reading and scowled at her. "That newspaper is of no use to me, but just what do you think you'd do with it?"

8

Frances stood as tall and straight as she could. Stupid man! What did he think she would do? "I would read it," she said firmly.

He laughed loudly, then jeered, "Read it? Ha! As if you urchins could read! Toss it over there—in that basket." He reached for the inkwell and soon was penning an answer to Mr. Lomax's letter.

I hate you! Frances thought as she followed his orders. *You're a fat, horrible bully! Who are you to decide whether I can or can't read? You don't know me!* She clenched her fists, wishing she could speak the words aloud.

She still treasured the memory of when she was a very little girl and Da had held her on his lap, the newspaper before them.

"What's this word?" she'd asked, pointing. "And this one?" she'd insist as soon as he answered. "And this one?"

"Ah, Frances Mary," Da had said one day, "I think you're after learnin' to read."

She had nodded vigorously. "Teach me to read, Da," she had begged, so he did. She loved to read and was proud of her reading because it was pleasing to Da.

Since they were unable to afford the clothes or books that sending the little ones to school demanded, Frances had tried to pass on her father's teaching to the others. Mike had learned eagerly, gulping in words as hungrily as he gulped in food at supper. Danny had learned, too, following Mike's example; but after a few mistakes, Megan had hung back, unsure of herself, and could read very little.

Mr. Waterfield suddenly stood up, breaking into Frances's thoughts. He tucked his sheet of paper into an envelope and held it out. "Get this answer to Mr. Lomax right away," he snapped. "And no dawdling!"

9

"Yes, sir," Frances said. Still furious, she took the envelope, threw open the door, and ran down the hallway to the street. She walked briskly, this time able to notice the people around her. There were gentlemen dressed in ankle-length topcoats that swung around their legs as they walked. Many of them wore top hats and carried canes, some with heads of polished silver. The women wore long coats or capes that covered their full skirts almost to the hems. Most wore gloves, but a few had tucked their hands inside fur muffs. Tilted over their foreheads were hats, decorated with silk flowers and tied under their chins with matching ribbons.

A woman brushed past her, sweeping her skirts out of the way. Her snug-waisted, bottle-green coat was fastened by a row of jet-black buttons that winked and sparkled as they caught the light. *Wouldn't Ma, with her red hair, look grand in a coat like that!* thought Frances. In her mind, she could see her mother, tall and elegant, with the skirt of her coat swirling regally around her legs as she walked. Frances ached as she thought of Ma's patched and faded clothes and shabby shawl. She wished with all her heart that she could buy a bottle-green coat for her mother, but she knew that a coat like that would cost much more than all the money she made in a month.

Near the intersection of Fifth and Broadway, Frances nearly bumped into a girl of her own size who was looking into a shop window. The girl wore a flared, pale blue velvet coat and matching bonnet, and her hands were tucked into a white fur muff.

"Look, Mama," the girl said to the woman who stood next to her. "Look at the doll in the pink dress."

Frances looked, too, at a doll with a creamy china face and blue glass eyes, dressed in a pink silk dress made with dozens of tiny tucks and pleats and trimmed with ribbon rosettes. Frances gasped aloud. "Oh! The wonder of her!"

The girl in blue glanced at Frances and smiled. For an instant they shared the same delight in the elegant doll. But the woman turned toward Frances with a look of horror and disgust. She tugged at the girl's hand, yanking her away. She whispered to the girl, but Frances could catch some of the words: ". . . do not talk to one of *those* children."

Frances turned away from them, burning with humiliation. She stared with frustration at her own reflection in the window, seeing what the woman had seen: a barefoot girl with tattered, mud-splattered clothing. *It's not fair*, Frances cried to herself. She rested her forehead against the cold glass, embarrassment erupting into hot tears that ran down her cheeks. She hated being so poor. It wasn't her fault.

A rough hand gripped her shoulder and spun her around. A policeman demanded, "What mischief might you be up to?"

Frances stiffened with fear. "No mischief," she managed to stammer.

His voice softened as he saw her tears. "Then be along with you, girl! Go about your business! Don't dawdle here with your betters where you don't belong."

Frances turned and broke into a run. Why should she be treated as though she had done something wrong? Wasn't she allowed even to stop and rest? Her betters? Just because they wore nicer clothes? "It's not fair!" she sobbed aloud.

"Look where you're going!" a top-hatted gentleman barked at her.

She stumbled against the cane he thrust out, then

angrily turned and grabbed it from his hand, tossing it to the ground.

"How dare you—you!" he sputtered, but Frances ran on.

Heedlessly she dashed across streets, ignoring the clang of wagon and cab wheels against the cobblestones and the angry shouts of drivers. She darted through clusters of peddlers and shoppers as she hurried back to her job. Her chest hurt, and her stomach churned with shame and anger. All she wanted was to be with her mother. Ma, with her smiles and loving words, would make everything right again.

By the time she reached Mr. Lomax's office, Frances was out of breath, but calmer. She delivered Mr. Waterfield's reply, then hurried from Mr. Lomax's office, thankful that he had made no mention of docking her wages again.

She hurried to find her mother. She knew that Ma would be already hard at work rubbing the brass on the ornate staircase that rose from the lobby to the second story of the office building on Twenty-third Street. The narrow, two-story building was not as elegant on the outside as those in Mr. Waterfield's neighborhood; but its sweeping, curved marble staircase and brass-trimmed, teakwood balusters and balustrade made up for it.

Ma swept some flyaway strands of hair from her eyes, looked up, and smiled at Frances, then blinked with surprise. "Frances Mary, it's wet and cold you are!"

Frances crouched beside her mother, who wrapped her arms around her daughter, briskly rubbing her back and shoulders. "A cab wheel hit a puddle," Frances said. "No harm. The running kept me warm."

"Better now?" Ma leaned back and smiled.

"Much," Frances said. There wasn't time to tell her mother how much warmer she felt just being near her, so she reached to squeeze Ma's strong, firm hands.

Frances thought again about the beautiful green coat, and she clutched her mother's hands more tightly. Ma would be the first to say she would have no need for a fancy coat like that, but Frances knew that what Ma needed and what she deserved to have were not the same. Then the memory of the girl in the pale blue coat and the words her mother had whispered sprang unbidden to Frances's mind.

Ma looked at Frances intently. "What is it, love?" she asked. "You look troubled. Is there something you'd like to tell me?"

Frances tried to smile as she quickly shook her head. She wouldn't want her mother to share the hurt and shame she'd felt. "No, Ma, nothing," she answered.

Behind Frances a voice spit out words as though they had a bad taste. It wasn't difficult to recognize fat Mrs. Watts. "Ah, Mrs. Kelly, your girl has finally returned. Well, if she soon gets busy it will make the work load a little lighter for the rest of us."

"Hold your tongue, Mrs. Watts," Ma said. "You know Frances Mary was sent off on an errand for Mr. Lomax."

"She's back now, ain't she? And I don't see her jumping in to pull her fair share."

Frances quickly snatched a rag from the pile next to her mother, scooted down to the bottom stair, and began rubbing hard on the brass curlicues in the hard-to-reach places on the balusters. With a grunt, Mrs. Watts picked up a bucket and scrub brush and began to waddle up the stairs, her mouth still puckered as though she had bitten into a sour pickle. When she was sure Mrs. Watts would not look back, Ma puffed out her cheeks, pursed her lips, and waggled her head in imitation. Frances tried not to laugh aloud. She had learned not to mind Mrs. Watts's sharp remarks. As Ma had said, "The woman sees only the dark side of life, and for that we should pity her."

From the circular window over the double front doors, Frances watched a deep blue twilight begin to settle over the city. Soon a lamplighter began his rounds, creating yellow puddles of light. The last few office workers hurried down the steps, chatting with one another, ignoring Frances and her mother. The heavy outer doors clanged behind them, but the lobby echoed their voices after they had gone.

Frances polished and scrubbed, lugging the heavy bucket of water step-by-step to the top floor. She rubbed the desks with a soft cloth and swept the day's layer of soot and grime from the carpets.

While her body worked, her thoughts escaped to the special place her imagination had built. It was a beautiful red brick house in which Ma and Da and all Frances's brothers and sisters lived. Its windows looked out over a vast green lawn and a shimmering blue lake that was much like the lake in Ireland Da had described so often. The living room of the house was decorated with embroidered pillows and cotton lace curtains, like a room that Frances had once seen through lighted windows at night. On an elegant, scrolled table next to the davenport, a basket of piping-hot loaves of bread sat next to a bowl of juicy oranges and tart, crisp apples. Remembering the pungent cheese in Mr. Waterfield's office, Frances smiled as she mentally added a large wedge of it to the center of the table. Behind the davenport, she built a high case of shelves and filled it with books of all sizes and colors.

Frances pictured Megan cradling the doll in the pink

silk dress, while Mike leaned over the table, munching and reading, so captivated by his book that he ignored the apple juice dribbling down his chin. Da sat with Petey on one knee, while Peg and Danny played a noisy game of touch tag. The door flew open, and in came Ma, gorgeous in her green coat, her arms filled with packages. She smiled and laughed as she greeted them, and the children ran to her to be hugged. She tossed her packages on the nearby chair.

Frances giggled as her imagination added a whole new scene to the daydream.

"Mr. Waterfield," Ma called. "Please put away these packages for me." A woebegone Mr. Waterfield got up from scrubbing the floor on his knees and hurried to do what Ma had asked. "And, Mr. Waterfield," she said, "when you've finished with that chore, I'd like you to—"

Her mother broke into Frances's dream by taking the broom from her hands and locking it into the closet where the cleaning tools were kept. "Nearly midnight. Time for home and bed," Ma said.

She smiled as she took their shawls from a hook and handed the smaller one to Frances, but Frances could see the dark smudges under her mother's eyes.

Ma clasped Frances's hand in her warm, rough, right hand. With her left hand she opened the side door, pushing hard against the wind. Clutching her shawl tightly, head down against the wind, Frances ran to keep pace with Ma's long stride.

Frances knew that life had always been hard for her mother. She had left Ireland when she was twenty-one and newly married, with her husband, who was twenty-six. "No one would ever choose to leave that blessed land," Ma had told Frances, "but the brutal fact was that we would have starved if we'd stayed there. The potato

15

crops had rotted in the ground, and as time went on the situation grew worse. There just was not enough food to feed everyone, so many people had to leave the country. Your father and I thought long and hard about our choice. We thought about the life we wanted for our children. Then we said good-bye to our family and friends and came to the United States."

"Oh, Ma! How could you leave your family? I'd die if I thought I'd never see you again!" Frances hated this part of the story, feeling the terrible loneliness that had crept into her mother's words.

Ma had answered matter-of-factly, "Sometimes we must do what needs to be done, and that's the all of it."

Often Ma spoke of the beautiful Bens, the row of mountains that stood like sentinels watching over her homeland. Frances thought Ma was like the Bens, as steady and never-changing as those mountains she loved. It was not until that terrible year when Da died of the lung sickness that Frances saw another side of her mother.

For as long as Frances could remember, Da had worked long hours, climbing ladders up the walls of buildings under construction with loads of bricks on the hod, or wooden trough, that rested on his shoulder. With a trowel he would spread the bricks with mortar, smoothing them into place, then climb down and back with another load. The muscles in Da's arms were thick and firm, and his skin was browned from the sun. And when he came home each night, he was never too tired to lift the children high overhead, while his loud laughter bounced from the walls of the room.

Then, suddenly, he became ill and weak. The hospital doctors did all that they could, then sent him home, telling Ma to spoon-feed him a mixture of pulverized beef bones mixed with red wine. Ma did everything she

---

16

could to care for him, and Frances helped, too, but each day Da grew more pale and shrunken in the bed. Frances, terrified and heartbroken, unable to believe how Da had changed, would hold his hand and whisper, "Please get well, Da! Please!" She'd tell him the stories that he had told her about Ireland, the green and golden country she had learned to love. "We'll go to visit someday when you're better," she promised, but Da's health did not improve.

One morning Ma gently folded Da's hands across his chest, pulled the sheet up to cover his face, and called the children together. She told them that their father was dead.

Sometimes during the waking hours of the night, Frances still would be swept with the memory of the hurt and anger and wild tears that tore through her body like sharp claws. Even though she was the eldest, her own tears had left her so weak that she had no will to help comfort the others who wailed for their father. But Ma had remained strong and found room for all of them in her arms. With an energy that burnished her skin, Ma had taken care of the funeral arrangements, using what little money they'd been able to save. Then Ma had found cleaning jobs for Frances and herself in the office building managed by Mr. Lomax.

"It's not what we wanted for you, love, but I know I can count on you," Ma had murmured. "I promised your Da this family would never starve." Frances had hugged her mother in response.

"I *want* to work with you," she insisted. "We'll take care of the little ones together, Ma."

But one night, nearly a week after Da's coffin had been laid in the ground, Frances had awakened from a heavy sleep. It was that time of night in which darkness fades to gray, and shadows loom, and it's hard to know what is real and what is not. Then, for the first time, Frances heard her mother cry.

Little Pete and Peg were sleeping crossways in the one big bed in which all the children slept, Pete's thumb in his mouth, Peg murmuring in her sleep. But Mike, Danny, and Megan crouched together at one end of the bed, their eyes wide with fear.

Frances had slipped quickly from the bed and stumbled to the cot on which her mother lay. "Ma! Ma! You mustn't cry!" she pleaded. "I've never seen you cry like this, Ma! Please don't cry!"

Her mother's only answer was to moan through her tears, "Tom, Tom, Tom."

"What should I do?" Frances cried aloud, but there was no answer. Shivering more from fear than from cold, she huddled against Ma, wrapping her arms around her, and Ma curled into them like a small child. Terrified, Frances held her mother through the storm of sobs and wails, then lifted the edge of her own nightgown to dry her mother's eyes. She stroked her hair and soothed her until Ma fell asleep.

But Frances lay awake long after, until the sky was streaked with light. Her frantic fears had subsided into a lump of cold that ached in the pit of her stomach. Frances knew that things would never be the same. She was no longer a little girl; those moments had forced her into a world of adult responsibility, and there was no turning back.

Ma never spoke of it, and Frances couldn't put into words what she had learned during the night, but she was comforted by the knowledge that the bond between them had grown even stronger.

Now, as they walked home together, Frances and her

mother crossed over to Ninth Avenue, going south, on streets in which the traffic had thinned. The rows of small greengrocers, meat markets, haberdasheries, and dry-goods stores were closed, their stained and faded canvas awnings cranked up tightly. The peddlers' carts had vanished, relegated to wherever they were stored for the night, but spoiled fruit and wilted cabbage leaves still littered the curbs.

In spite of the hour, the streets teemed with people. Some of them sat on stoops or leaned against the corner gaslights. Frances shot quick glances at them. Many were boys, some no older than Danny or Peg. There were gangs of thieves in their neighborhood, but she knew they wouldn't try to rob a pair of poor cleaning women. It was obvious that Frances and her mother carried nothing of value. Frances kept a lookout, but she wasn't afraid. Mike had taught her well how to handle herself. "Too well," he had grumbled after their last lesson as he held a rag to his own bloody nose.

As they turned onto Sixteenth Street, which cut through rows of crowded tenements, Frances thought she saw a familiar figure ahead of them. Mike? What would Mike be doing out so late? Rapidly the figure slipped into the doorway of the building in which the Kellys lived.

Frances quickened her step and entered the building ahead of her mother, wrinkling her nose in disgust as the familiar stench of cooking odors, garbage, and unwashed bodies that clung to the walls of the long, narrow hallway surrounded them like a smothering gray ghost.

As Ma quietly opened the door to the room that was their home, Frances thought she heard a low groan. She glanced in the direction of the room next to theirs where her friend, Mara Robi, lived with her aunt and uncle.

Through the cracks around the door she could see the flicker of candlelight. Mara had been ill with a cough and fever. Maybe she was worse.

"Ma," Frances whispered, and clutched her mother's arm. "That could be Mara! Come with me!"

Ma murmured, "It's late. You can visit Mara tomorrow."

"But what if she needs—"

"Hush," Ma said, patting her shoulder. "She has her uncle and aunt to care for her, and you need your sleep."

Frances hung her shawl on a hook as her mother lit the small whale-oil lamp that stood on the table in the center of the room. The glass of the lamp shimmered as the store window had, and Frances shuddered as she remembered her ragged, dirty reflection. But she looked around at the clean, spare furnishings in their room with pride: a few straight-backed wooden chairs, a table on which lay a Bible and a small framed wedding picture of Da and Ma, a double bed for the children to share, a cot for Ma, a small wood-burning stove in the corner, and floors scrubbed so clean the wood was bleached nearly white. Ma was bending over the sleeping children, a smile on her face. Frances knew that Ma wanted better for them. That they had so little was not her fault.

Frances glanced at her brothers and sisters, automatically checking to see that all were safe and accounted for. Dark-haired, fragile Megan—who at the age of twelve had the job of caring for the little ones—was deep in sleep; seven-year-old Peg, with her bouncy red curls and splash of freckles, snuggled on Megan's arm. As usual young Petey, a curly-haired, blue-eyed six-year-old, had managed to work his way crossways in the bed, his feet almost in Danny's face. Redheaded Mike, one year older than ten-year-old Danny, who was almost his carbon copy, lay sprawled on his face, breathing heavily.

Too heavily, Frances thought, and she stood by the bed silently listening and watching. She recognized the uneven breathing of someone who has been running hard, and suddenly she was sure that she saw one of Mike's eyes flick open for an instant's peek before it was squeezed shut again. Ha! She'd been right! That *had* been Mike dashing home ahead of them.

Ma had already splashed her face and arms in the bowl of water that stood on the corner stand. She looked up from the cloth she had dried herself with and whispered, "Get a move on, Frances. You haven't washed yet."

"I will, Ma," Frances answered.

Knowing Mike, she supposed he'd been out causing a little mischief. Smiling at her brother, she shook her head and whispered, "Just you wait until morning! Like it or not, Mike, my boy, I'm going to find out what you've been up to!"

3

FRANCES AWOKE WITH the pale sunlight that filtered through the room's one small window. There was no time to lie in bed, clinging to dreams. Too much had to be done.

As Frances sat on the edge of the bed, blinking sleep from her eyes, Megan smiled at her. Gentle Megan, as usual, was first up, already dressed and tending to breakfast. Frances smiled back, thinking how peacefully reassuring it was that every morning repeated itself over and over.

As soon as they had eaten—either slabs of heavy Irish soda bread or a porridge that simmered on the stove until it was thick—Megan would carry her basket to the greengrocer's to buy potatoes and cabbage, which would be boiled for the noon meal.

Danny and Mike, with their shoeshining kits, would head uptown to the streets of office buildings, where well-dressed businessmen, on their way to work, might take time to let one of the "shiners" polish their shoes.

Ma would open the box of shirts to be sewn, and she and Frances would pull their straight, wooden chairs to the window to catch the light in order to sew the tiny stitches demanded by the tailor who paid them to work on this piecework. Frances liked to sew with her mother, enjoying the closeness, the stories Ma would sometimes tell, and especially the songs she'd sing in a voice as soft and comforting as a newly knit shawl.

Even the little ones, Peg and Petey, had their chores, tidying, dusting, drying the tin plates and utensils. Ma demanded cleanliness in and about the room and of all who lived in it. Each week the children carried buckets of water from the trough in the hall, and Ma would heat it by the kettleful to fill the large round tub that stood on end in the corner behind the stove, until everyone had bathed.

Frances held up her dress. Would it need an extra washing with the lye soap Ma had made? It had dried, and she rubbed the skirt briskly, dusting away the streaks of mud. When she was satisfied that the stains from her drenching the day before no longer showed, she hurried into a corner of the room, dressed quickly, and brushed her long dark hair, loving the soft heaviness of it as it spilled over her hands. Frances was proud of her hair, because Ma loved it. "So dark and fine, like my own mother's hair," Ma had said.

As she came to the table, Mike was reading a tattered copy of a dime novel, *Seth Jones, Or Captive of the Frontier*. He looked up at Frances and said, "Now this is an exciting story! If you want to read it again, you'll have to wait."

Frances laughed. "I've read it and I told you, I don't

23

like the story much. I don't want to read about the frontier." She dropped into the nearest chair. Petey immediately crawled on her lap, and Frances nuzzled his cropped blond curls.

"I don't understand you," Mike said. "The frontier's exciting! I've heard the tales about wide open spaces filled with herds of deer and buffalo! Think of this—each man has his own horse and can ride for miles and miles without seeing a single building! And there are Indians who ride wild horses and gallop down from the hills, whooping and hollering! I'd like that, I would!"

Frances sniffed. "Huh! If all that is true, then the West, with all its wild ways, is a place where I'm never going to be, and you can bet on that!"

Mike plopped his empty bowl onto the table and picked up his shine kit. "Off to meet the swells!" he said. "Let's hope the dust from yesterday's wind dirtied a lot of boots."

Ma smiled. Mike, whose infectious grin was as bright as his tousled red hair, could always make her smile.

"Wait for me," Danny cried through a mouthful of gruel.

"Hurry up, then," Mike said. He pulled on his jacket and cap as he walked toward the door. Although Danny was an inch taller than Mike, who was small for his age, Mike, as older brother, had no trouble keeping Danny in line.

Now was Frances's chance. She slipped up behind Mike and pushed him into the hallway, quietly shutting the door behind her. "I have to talk to you, Mike," she said. "I want to ask you a question."

He grinned. "If you're lucky, I'll give you an answer."

"It's about last night. You got home just before Ma and me. She didn't see you, but I did."

"When you came in, I was sleeping soundly."

"I saw you open one eye."

Mike pretended to look surprised. "One eye, was it? Then tell me, what was the other eye doing all this while?"

Frances couldn't keep from giggling. "Mike," she said, "be serious."

Danny rushed into the hallway so fast he almost collided with Frances. "I'm ready, Mike!" he shouted. Danny was barefoot, as Mike was, and he had no jacket to wear over his shirt and knickers, having grown so fast during the summer he couldn't fit into the only one he owned. Danny looked from Mike to Frances. "What are you two talking about?"

"Nothing," Mike said.

But Frances was not going to be put off. "Danny," she said, "do you know where Mike was last night?"

The guilt on Danny's face was as thick as jam as he answered, "Wasn't he home in bed?"

Frances sighed. She'd get nowhere with Danny. After Da had died, Danny had clung to Mike as though he were a father. "In bed is where Mike should have been," Frances said.

"And isn't that where you found me?" Mike looked at her with wide-eyed innocence.

Frances pretended to scowl, but she couldn't keep the smile from her lips. She was much too fond of Mike ever to be angry with him. "You think you can talk yourself out of anything!" she called after Mike, as she watched her brothers run down the hallway and out the front door of the building, but she wondered with a shivering doubt about his ability to talk his way out of *everything*.

Frances hesitated a moment outside the room where

Mara lived. People were up and about, as she knew they would be. Mara's Uncle Gerik opened the door to Frances's knock. He was a ragpicker by trade, who searched through scraps and gutters for rags, then washed and sold them. By this time he should have been out on the streets with his cart.

"How is Mara? Please don't tell me that she's worse!" Frances stammered.

As Uncle Gerik's eyes shifted to avoid Frances's gaze, she frantically squirmed past him and into the room. The Robis had even less furniture than the Kellys, and the bare wooden floor of their room was dusty with lint from the piles of rags in every corner.

Mara, who lay on a small pallet, was covered with a thin, dirty blanket. Her dark hair was so damp it was plastered to her skull as though it had been painted there, and her cheeks were red and flushed. Frances gasped. The smell of illness, so strong in spite of the thick stench of garlic in the air, carried her back to the terror and pain of when Da had been so ill. She hurried to Mara's side, kneeling beside her. "Do you have medicine for her?" Frances asked.

"Good soup make better," Aunt Annuska said. She tried for more words, but her English was not very good. She held up some piecework she had laid across Mara's pallet. "Better soon. Then she can sew. Much work to do." She glanced at Mara as though the girl were lazy and taking an unearned rest.

"Soup is not enough," Frances said firmly. She could see the watery brown liquid that was simmering in an iron pot on the Robis' stove. She took Mara's hand, but it was damp and limp, as Da's hand had been. Suddenly terrified, Frances jumped to her feet and shouted, "She should go to the hospital where a doctor could care for her!"

Mara's aunt and uncle began to speak rapidly in a language Frances couldn't understand. It was easy to tell, however, that they were frightened of the hospital—where so many sick people were taken, never to return—and of doctors—who would demand money in exchange for medicine. How could she make them understand that Mara needed more help than they could give her?

Next to Megan, Mara was Frances's best friend. The day the Kellys moved into this building, Mara had approached Frances with a shy smile and a knotted string and invited her to share a game of cat's cradle. Since then they had talked and walked and played together whenever they could leave work behind long enough.

Fiercely determined that she would not lose Mara, Frances ignored the Robis and bent over her friend. "Do you want to go to the hospital where the doctor will help you?" she asked.

Mara was barely able to nod her head.

Ignoring the excited chatter of Uncle Gerik and Aunt Annuska, Frances rushed from the room. As she ran into her own home, her heart was beating so hard it pounded in her ears, but she managed to stammer, "Mara's very sick, Ma! I'm afraid! Please help her!"

Ma nodded. Without a word she stood, pulled on her shawl, and left the room.

While Ma was gone, Frances tried to work on the shirt she was sewing, but her fingers trembled, and she had to rip out many stitches. Megan hushed the little ones and tried to comfort Frances, saying, "You know Ma. She'll find someone who will help."

Frances somehow had finished stitching in both sleeves and had almost completed the tightly rolled hem by the time she again heard voices and footsteps in the hall. The door to the Robis' room opened and shut, Aunt

Annuska's wails burst through the wall, and voices rumbled in anger. Soon the door opened and shut again, and footsteps hurried down the hall. Frances and Megan waited, desperate to know what had taken place, yet fearful to find out.

Ma calmly came through the door and hung up her shawl. "Mara is very ill," she said, "but the doctor said the illness has not reached her lungs, and with care and good food she'll get better soon." She paused. "He had her carried to the hospital."

Frances felt her legs wobble, and she sat on the nearest chair. "Will she be back home soon?"

Ma put an arm around Frances's shoulder. After a while she spoke quietly and slowly, as though many words were laid out before her and she was choosing among them carefully. "A man came with the doctor. He's a minister. His name is Charles Loring Brace, and he has set up something called the Children's Aid Society, which cares for needy children. The doctor and Reverend Brace think that Mara will do better if she stays for a while at the home the Society has set up for orphaned children." Frances's mother glanced at her and quickly added, "Just till she's well again."

"Is that why Aunt Annuska was yelling so loudly?" Megan asked.

Ma nodded. "It took a little while to convince Annuska and Gerik that this was for the best." She was silent for a moment, then added thoughtfully, "I've seen Reverend Brace in this neighborhood before, and I've heard only good about the orphaned children he places out in new homes in the West, where there's plenty of fresh food and clean air and warm clothing to be had."

Frances was sorry for the poor, parentless children Reverend Brace had sent to the West—and desperately thankful that she wasn't one of them. How awful to be taken away from friends—maybe even other family members—to the wild, terrifying frontier that Mike had described. She gasped as she realized that Mara *was* an orphan! And now she was in Reverend Brace's care. Frances shivered against a cold, creeping guilt. What had she done to her friend? "Ma," she asked, "was Mara frightened about being taken away from her aunt and uncle?"

"Mara will be all right," Ma said. She crossed to her chair, sat down, and picked up the shirtsleeve on which she had been working. As she bent over it and began again a row of tiny stitches, she added, "Mara needed to be cared for, love, and that's the all of it."

"I would have helped care for her, Ma," Frances insisted.

"She needed more care than you or I could give," Ma said.

Frances picked up her piecework and bent over it, trying to see the stitches through a blur of tears. "I didn't get to say good-bye," she whispered.

She worked steadily, unaware that Megan had begun to cook the noon meal until Mike and Danny burst through the door, dropping their shine kits and stirring like a whirlwind the fragrance of potatoes and cabbage that filled the room.

"I'm hungry, Ma!" Danny called.

"You're always hungry!" Mike shoved him, laughing and diving over the bed as Danny chased him.

Smoothing her skirt, Ma stood up. "Pull the chairs to the table," she said. "I'll help Megan dish up."

Danny fished into his pocket, pulled out a few coins, and dropped them onto the table. "Mike was right," he said with a grin. "Lots of dusty boots this morning."

Mike emptied his own pockets, and, along with the coins he'd earned, a shining, pearl-handled pocketknife fell onto the table.

"Ohhh!" Peg said, grabbing for the knife. "Where did you get this?"

Mike was quicker than Peg, and the knife disappeared into his pocket. "Found it," he said. "Some swell must have dropped it, and I was lucky."

"You were *indeed* lucky," Ma said as she ladled food onto the plates, but Frances had seen the wary look in Danny's eyes and knew Mike hadn't found that knife.

She sat down slowly, trying to think. Surely Mike wouldn't have stolen it. Da had taught all the children, over and over, that thievery was a crime. Mike had said he had found the knife. Frances wanted to believe him, but she couldn't help doubting his word. As she ate, she sneaked a sideways glance at Mike now and then, until he finally turned toward her and stuck out his tongue.

The promise she made to herself was just as solemn as if she'd spoken it aloud: *All right, Michael Patrick Kelly, that does it! Whether you like it or not, I'll find out just what it is you're up to!*

After their meal, Ma folded two of the shirts carefully and wrapped them in the brown paper in which they'd arrived. "Will you take these to Mr. Totts, Frances? It will give you a little rest from the sewing. Just come home before four so we can be at work on time."

Mike immediately declared that he had to get back to shining, and Danny scurried through the door on Mike's heels.

This is my chance, Frances thought. She was the eldest in the family. If Mike were doing something that might get him into trouble, then she should find out and

30

put a stop to it. Giving her brothers just enough time to leave the building, she raced down the hall and out to the street, so that she could follow them at a safe distance.

As they traveled uptown, Frances dodged and squeezed in and out among women with shopping baskets on their arms, peddlers making sales, and barrels of salted fish, pickles, and crackers lining the sidewalk under store-keepers' awnings. The midday streets were noisy and crowded, and Frances had to scramble to keep from losing sight of her brothers. "Why did I start this?" she muttered to herself; but she had, and she was stubbornly determined to stick to her task. She followed the boys for blocks, until they reached a neighborhood of fine stores, restaurants, and hotels. But she halted as she saw Mike stop to say something to Danny, then point north along Broadway. Obviously Mike was sending Danny away, and Danny was reluctant to go.

He finally did go, and Frances moved in closer, keeping a sharp eye on Mike. Suddenly he slipped into an alley.

Frances trailed him cautiously, ducking behind a stack of barrels, moving ahead only when she was sure he hadn't seen her. She squatted behind a large wooden packing box. If she looked through one of its torn slats, she could watch Mike. He was pressed against the rough brick wall, his eyes on the building across the street.

Frances shivered. The dark alley sucked in gusts of the cold wind and spit out swirls of dust, pebbles, and scraps of paper. Frances saw Mike shiver, too, and rub one bare foot on top of the other.

"Hssst, Mike!"

The whisper startled Frances as much as it did Mike. She stuffed a hand against her mouth, trying not to cry out. Mike instinctively jumped to one side, crouching, fists up.

31

The whisperer appeared from behind a large barrel. "Mike, it's me, Danny."

"I told you not to follow me!" Mike said. Grabbing Danny's shoulders, Mike shook him furiously. "Don't ever creep up on me like that!"

Danny trembled as another gust of wind rattled through the alley. "It's cold here," Danny complained.

Mike peeled off his thin coat and handed it to Danny. "Put this on and get away from here."

Danny didn't argue. He dove into the coat and stretched it across his chest, tucking his chin down into what was left of the collar. "I want to stay with you," he said.

"No, you don't," Mike told him firmly. "I've got work to do, and I don't want you around getting in the way."

"I could watch you and learn," Danny pleaded. He paused and glanced around carefully. Frances held her breath and tried to shrink back even farther into the shadows, relieved that Danny didn't see her. Danny turned back to Mike and lowered his voice, but Frances could hear every word. "You're a copper stealer, aren't you, Mike?"

Frances held a hand over her mouth, stifling a sob. So Mike was a thief! And Danny, because he idolized his older brother, wanted to be a copper stealer, too.

Frances took a step forward, ready to run into the alley and give her brothers a good, strong piece of her mind; but Mike angrily grabbed Danny, turned him around, and gave him a shove. "None of your business!" he hissed. "Get out of here! I mean it!"

Flinching like a hurt pup, Danny ran back the way he had come, and once again Frances saw Mike position himself against the wall, staring intently at the impressive building. She knew the building. Inside was an elegant restaurant. Frances started toward Mike, then paused. If she confronted Mike with a threat to tell Ma what he was doing, would he listen, or would he try to shove her away, as he had done to Danny?

Before Frances could decide, a large door swung open across the street, and a group of gentlemen in greatcoats and top hats, loudly talking and laughing, sauntered from the restaurant. Mike crouched like a runner before a race. Oh, no! Frances knew what he was going to do! She tried to shout, but the words grated against her throat like sharp-edged stones.

A cab driver clucked to his horse, which clopped toward the group, and the men moved toward the street.

"Now!" Mike said aloud and dashed from the alley into the street. He dodged carriage wheels and the hooves of passing horses and the whips of angry drivers. Terrified, Frances ran after him.

She saw Mike slam into the group of men who still stood in front of the restaurant. He bounced off the rounded belly of a portly gentleman who was struggling with the long ends of a heavy muffler, trying unsuccessfully to fasten his greatcoat. For an instant the two of them were locked together, twirling and staggering, until the man tottered back, off-balance, his black moustache quivering with indignation. He shouted and waved a fist at Mike, who gave him one last glance before racing around the corner.

Less than a block away Mike dove into another alley. When Frances arrived at the alley, out of breath and gulping for air, he was gone. She was frantic that she had lost him until she heard a scrabbling noise and a chuckle coming from a pile of discarded packing boxes. As quietly as she could, she climbed high enough to look down at Mike, who was sitting in a nest of rags and a bright piece of woolen scarf. He had opened his fist, and inside it lay a wad of bills and a gold money clip.

"Oh, Mike!" Frances cried out, sick at her discovery. "How could you!"

Mike tried to jump up, but fell back, legs flailing desperately as he fought to regain his balance. "What are you doing here?" he yelled at Frances. "You've got no business scaring me like that!"

"You stole that man's money!" Frances gasped.

Mike scrambled out of his nest so quickly that he knocked Frances off-balance. The two of them staggered, grabbing at each other to steady themselves, before Mike snapped, "I've stolen before. Lots of times."

Frances cried out, "But stealing is wrong!"

"Is it, now!" Mike glared at his sister defensively. Frances had never heard this bitter tone in his voice before.

"You know it is! Can't you remember Da telling you so?"

Mike snapped back, "Did Da ever say that stealing was wrong when it meant not going hungry?"

Frances pressed a hand against her stomach. She well knew what it was to be hungry; she knew about people—like those gentlemen—who had more food than they could ever eat, while others went to bed at night with their empty bellies aching. But she also knew what was right—what Da had taught her. Those smiling eyes and that firm voice hadn't lied.

"Stealing for any reason is wrong, Mike," Frances said.

Mike raised his chin even higher. "You've eaten the meat I've been able to bring home now and then. Ma's wearing shoes I bought for her with money I've stolen."

"She doesn't know." Frances's voice was just a whisper.

For an instant there was pain in Mike's eyes, and his

voice softened. "I don't like to steal, Frances," he admitted, "but I haven't got a choice. You see that, don't you?"

The words burned her throat, but Frances said, "I can't, Mike! It's wrong and it's untrue to Da!"

"Da didn't know how hard it would be for Ma and the rest of us to earn enough to live on after he left us!"

"Mike!" she cried. "It wasn't his fault!"

"He left us to make our way alone! Without him! And it's none of your business what I do! You're not in charge of me!"

"I'm not going to let you steal!" she insisted, fighting anger and hurt and a wild desire to shake her brother until his teeth rattled.

"It doesn't matter," Mike said. His bravado deserted him as he slumped against the pile of boxes. "It's something I've got to do."

Frances ached for him. Tentatively, she reached out, then quickly pulled back her hand. If she were going to help Mike, she'd have to remain firm. "You'll get caught," she told him.

"No, I won't," Mike insisted. "The lads say I'm too clever."

"What lads?"

"Bertie, Ted, Jack—you know them. We stick together."

A shadow suddenly fell over them, and Frances was shoved aside. She cried out in terror as a policeman's hand gripped Mike's shoulder tightly. "Is this the one?" he asked the man behind him.

It was the gentleman whom Mike had robbed. The man was so angry that his moustache trembled. "Yes! That's the little thief!" he shouted.

Frances took one look at Mike's panic-stricken face and stumbled forward, teeth chattering as she tried to

35

speak. "Please listen to me, sir!" She tugged at the man's sleeve, but he ignored her.

The policeman scowled at Frances and asked the gentleman, "How about the girl? Was she in it, too?"

As Frances gasped, Mike yelled, "No!" His face was so pinched and frightened that he looked like a shriveled old man. "She had nothing to do with this! She chased me! She tried to get me to give back the money!"

"Come with me, lad," the policeman said sternly. "You're under arrest."

Frances ran after them to the street, her thoughts a terrified jumble. What would happen to Mike? She had heard that copper stealers were sent to the crowded, filthy Tombs Prison. And Ma! Frances groaned aloud as she wondered how her mother would react.

"Frances!" Mike cried.

But there was nothing Frances could do to help him now.

4

As FRANCES FLUNG the door open with a crash and dashed into the room, Ma stared in amazement, first at Frances, then at the brown paper parcel she still held. "The shirts—?" she began, but Frances dropped the package and threw herself into her mother's arms.

"Oh, Ma!" she cried. "Something terrible happened, but don't get angry, please, Ma!"

Ma moved back, holding Frances by the shoulders so that she could look into her eyes, and said firmly, "Frances Mary, calm yourself, then tell me. What is it?" Ma's face was pale, but her gaze didn't waver.

"Mike's been arrested! He's a copper stealer!" Frances blurted out and burst into tears, barely managing to relate the entire story.

By the time she had finished her tale, Peg and Petey were wailing, and Megan's eyes were wide with horror.

Ma, her lips pale and tight, quickly wrapped her shawl

over her head and shoulders and strode toward the door. "I'll be going to the police station, Megan," she said. "You know what to do for the little ones."

"I'll come with you, Ma," Frances insisted.

"No," her mother told her. "Go to work as usual. Tell Mr. Lomax that I was detained by a family emergency and will be along later. That's all he needs to know." As Frances hesitated, Ma said, "You're a good, dependable girl, love. Do your job. We need the money."

Frances sat on the cot, helping Megan soothe and distract their little sister and brother.

"What will happen to Mike?" Megan murmured.

"I don't know," Frances said. "But everything will turn out all right, you'll see. Ma can take care of it."

Megan looked at her gratefully, and Frances wished she could have believed her own words. How could Ma, even with all her determination, keep Mike from being sent to Tombs Prison?

Later, while she scrubbed hard at the polished floors in the office building, under the watchful eye and sharp tongue of Mrs. Watts, Frances recalled what she had told Megan. She prayed that her words had been true, that Ma could make everything turn out all right. But the hours crept by, and still Ma didn't come. Frances jumped at every sound. She dropped her cleaning tools, forgot where she left her broom, and even spilled a bucket of scrub water. For that she took a tongue-lashing from Mrs. Watts. Where was Ma? What had happened?

Finally Frances jumped to her feet with a shout of relief as she saw Ma stride down the hallway of the office building, her bucket and brush in hand.

Ma stopped to lay a hand on Frances's shoulder. "Mike will be locked up for the night," she said in a low voice. "He'll go before the judge tomorrow morning at nine."

"Have you been at the police station all this while?" Frances whispered, clutching her mother's arms.

"No," Ma said. "I found Danny and sent him home. Then there was someone I had to talk to."

"About Mike?"

"Yes."

"Will Mike go to prison?"

For just a moment, Ma's eyes looked old and tired. "I pray not, love. If the judge will allow Mike to be helped—"

Frances interrupted. "But who will help Mike?"

"I'll tell you later, when it's the right time."

"Why not now?" Frances begged.

Ma pulled Frances to her and held her tightly. Against her hair she murmured, "Frances Mary, you'll have to trust me, no matter what happens. I'm asking you to be strong for me, to help me in what I must do. Just know that I love you with all my heart."

Frances shivered. The urgency in her mother's voice frightened her. "Ma," Frances pleaded, "let me go with you tomorrow. Please?"

She expected her mother to argue, but Ma simply said, "Yes. We will all be there."

Frances was comforted. She should have known that Ma would want them all on hand to help Mike. Of course they'd all be there.

Mrs. Watts, puffing with indignation, descended upon them, intent on informing the tardy Mrs. Kelly about her daughter's carelessness, and Frances hurried back to her job. As she scrubbed the dirty floors, she began to puzzle over Ma's words. What had she meant when she had asked for her trust? And whom had she called on for help? Nameless fears prickled under Frances's skin, and she shuddered, afraid again of what the next day might bring.

In the morning, as soon as everyone was dressed and fed, Ma asked Frances, "Will you take the children outside? I'll come to you when I'm ready."

Frances stared at her mother. "Why?" she asked. "What are you going to do? Can't you tell me?"

"I asked for your help," Ma reminded her. "Right now, the best help you can give me is to take the little ones out and keep an eye on them. Please trust me, Frances."

Frances nodded and reached for Petey's hand, leading the other children outside.

In about fifteen minutes Ma joined them. She carried a plump paper parcel wrapped tightly with string, and Frances eyed it suspiciously. The contents of that parcel must have something to do with Mike. It was soft and lumpy, as if it might contain clothes. Did that mean Ma thought Mike wouldn't be coming home with them? Oh! If only Ma would answer all her questions!

Together the Kelly family walked the many blocks to the city courthouse, then up the wide steps leading to its large outer doors. Frances was awed into silence by the high lobby ceiling with its ornate arches and by the many people who pushed and twisted past one another, hurrying in and out of the building. The children clung closely to their mother.

But Ma had spied someone over the heads of those around her, and she steered her family in the direction of a portly gentleman with a thick, dark beard and eyebrows to match. He smiled, then solemnly shook hands with each of the Kellys as Ma introduced them one by one.

"Children, this is Mr. Charles Loring Brace," Ma said. *The man who sends orphans out West!* Frances remembered his name with alarm. *How can he help Mike? Mike isn't an orphan.*

Frances studied Reverend Brace as he pulled a watch from the little pocket in front of his vest and glanced at it before tucking it back in place. Was he here to defend Mike? To keep him out of jail? She looked from him to her mother and shivered, suddenly cold with the suspicion that Reverend Brace could keep Mike out of jail in only one way—by sending him to live with a family in the West.

"Time to go to court," Reverend Brace said. "The room is in this direction."

"Ma?" Frances urgently tugged at her mother's skirt, but Ma shook her head for silence and followed Reverend Brace into the courtroom.

Frances wanted to plead with her mother, to beg her not to let Mike be sent away, but a calmer, inner voice kept reminding her that a new home for Mike would be much better than a cell in Tombs Prison. And hadn't Mike said over and over that he'd like to go west?

Most of the benches in the large, crowded courtroom were filled, but Reverend Brace found a place where the Kellys could squeeze in. Frances ducked her head a little and lifted Peg to her lap, glad for the chance to hold tightly to someone. Peg wasn't her usual energetic, independent self and snuggled gratefully against her sister. Megan sat between Frances and Ma, while Danny slumped unhappily on her left. Frances hurt almost as much for Danny as for Mike. He was heartbroken at what had happened to the brother he worshiped.

Men in dark, snugly buttoned suit coats and trousers, many of them wearing full beards that hid their high collars, talked to one another inside an area that was separated from the rows of seats by a low wooden railing. Against the far wall stood a high desk, and behind the desk sat the judge, who wore a black robe with full sleeves.

Suddenly the room was called to order. People either left the area or sat down, as a young man, dirty and ragged, was brought by uniformed officers to stand before the judge. As the accusation against him of assault and robbery in Gramercy Park was read aloud, Frances leaned forward to listen. Robbery. The same charge would be brought against Mike. But Mike wasn't a real thief like this one. With a sharp jolt of fear, Frances knew that others in the room would see no difference between Mike and this thief. After the charge had been read, the judge quickly conferred with two of the men who occasionally bent to whisper to accuser and accused, then soundly rapped his gavel on the desk as he loudly announced, "Five years in Tombs Prison."

Frances shivered as the man was led away and another one brought before the judge. Would Mike's future be decided by a decision this swift?

It took almost an hour by the big clock that hung on the side wall before Mike was led in. Petey, who had wiggled and squirmed before almost falling asleep on Ma's lap, jumped up and yelled, "Mike! There's Mike!"

Danny groaned aloud.

Mike looked at them, fear and shame in his face. The judge turned to scowl at Petey, and Ma quickly hushed him. Frances held her breath as the charges against Mike were read aloud. Megan's fingernails dug into the palm of her hand, but Frances didn't mind the pain. The still-angry gentleman whose pocket had been picked stood inside the railing and scowled at Mike.

"Your Honor, may I have your permission to approach the bench?" Reverend Brace stood at the railing, facing the judge.

"Ah, Reverend Brace again," the judge said. "I know how you collect ragamuffins, but don't tell me that you have come to speak a good word for this little thief?"

"I have come to ask for Michael Kelly," Reverend Brace answered. "As you know, Your Honor, it is my firm belief that these street children should have a chance at a new life with farm families in the West. I have talked to Michael's mother, and I sincerely believe that Michael is a good boy and was driven to thievery by the circumstances in which he lives."

Frances cried aloud, and several people in the courtroom turned to look at her. Her guess had been right. Mike was going to be sent away. She might never see her brother again!

The judge frowned. "We've heard this sermon before, Reverend Brace. You have your convictions, and I have mine. I feel that the best action to take with a boy who steals is to get him off the street." He picked up his gavel.

Suddenly Ma stood, and her voice rang out so loudly that the judge started. "Your Honor," she called, "may I please speak?" She continued without waiting for an answer. "It's easy to see that both you and Reverend Brace have the same idea. He wishes to take Michael off the street, too. It's just that Reverend Brace has a different way of going about it, sir."

Someone laughed. The judged blinked and looked hard at Ma, but she continued bravely. "Your Honor, sir, I have six fine children, but since my husband died last year our struggle has been difficult, and my children have been exposed to the temptations of the street. I have done my best, but it's unable I am to both feed them and protect them from danger." She paused and took a deep breath. "So I have asked Reverend Brace to send all my children west to be placed in homes with good people who can give them what I can't. Please, sir, it's begging you with all my heart I am that you allow Michael to go with his brothers and sisters."

Terrified, Frances cried out, "Ma! You can't!" But Ma, in her determination, ignored Frances, keeping her eyes on the judge.

Frances heard Danny try to smother a sob, while Peg, on Frances's lap, struggled to free herself, muttering, "Let me out!" Petey, who clung to Ma's skirt, stared with big eyes at Frances, his plump face beginning to reflect the look of horror she knew he must see on her own.

"Come down here, ma'am." The judge looked at the paper in front of him and added, "Mrs. Kelly."

As Ma tried to sidle past the children on the bench to reach the aisle, Peg jumped up to clasp her waist, and Petey grabbed her around the legs, wailing, "Ma! Don't leave me!"

"Frances, you promised!" Ma said, as she tried to break Petey's hold. "Help me now!"

"Bring the children with you," the judge ordered, "and quiet that boy."

Frances, numb with shock, automatically took charge of the children. Holding the sobbing Petey with one hand and Peg with the other, she followed her mother, Megan, and Danny down the aisle, through a gate in the railing, to a spot in front of the judge.

"Ouch!" Peg complained as she squirmed, trying to pull her hand from Frances's tight grasp. "You're hurting me!"

Megan reached for Peg, so Frances hoisted Petey into her arms and impatiently hissed, "You *must* be quiet!" Petey gulped back a fresh sob, but the tears continued to stream down his face.

Frances looked from the judge to her mother and back again, waiting for someone to say something. Ma's gaze didn't falter as she stood quietly, meeting the judge's look with shoulders back and chin held high.

The judge carefully studied each of the Kellys in turn, scowling and rubbing his chin as he tried to make up his mind.

It seemed forever before he finally turned to Reverend Brace. "Is all of what Mrs. Kelly told me true, to your knowledge, sir?"

"Yes, Your Honor," Reverend Brace said. "I have agreed to place all her children in new homes."

The judge hit his gavel on the desk with such force that Frances winced. "Then I hereby release Michael Kelly to your care." He scowled again, this time at Mike. "As for you, young man," he said, "if you do not prove worthy of a new home, if you must be sent back, then you'll find yourself residing in Tombs Prison with others of your kind!"

Before Ma could thank the judge, he waved them away and called for the next prisoner to be brought before him. They were shepherded out of the courtroom into the hallway, and soon an officer brought Mike to them.

"It's eternally grateful I am to you," Ma said to Reverend Brace. "Michael will prove your trust in him. Of that, I'm sure." She put a hand on Mike's shoulder. "I want your solemn promise, Michael Patrick Kelly, that you will never be a pickpocket again."

"I promise you, Ma," Mike said. "I already promised the same thing to myself." His chin began to tremble, and he flung himself against his mother, hugging her around the waist.

Ma thrust the parcel at Reverend Brace. "Here are their belongings. Mike's book, a few toys, some clothes." For a moment she seemed to falter. "They own very little."

"He's not taking us now, Ma! We're going home, aren't we?" Frances's heart pounded so loudly it made her dizzy. Reverend Brace rested a hand on her shoulder, but she jerked away from him.

Ma shook her head. "There's not time. Reverend Brace has arranged for you to join the children leaving today. Besides, it would be harder for all of us if you went home. It's much better this way." Her eyes shimmered as she added, "Believe me, love."

"No!" Frances shouted. "You can't do this!"

"Why are you sending us away?" Danny cried. "Is it because of what Mike did? He won't do it again, Ma. You heard him promise!"

"It's my fault. I'm this family's bad-luck penny," Megan whispered. She leaned against Frances and began to sob.

"It's not your fault! Ma's to blame!" Frances said, but Megan and Danny's outbursts of tears had set off the little ones, and no one heard her.

Ma tried to quiet Peg and Petey, who clung to her in desperation. She looked up to Frances. "Help me, love. Help me to make them understand."

"No!" Frances steeled herself against the hurt and astonishment in her mother's eyes. "I won't help you, because I don't understand, either!" Da's face suddenly came into her mind. He wouldn't have let this happen. It had nearly killed her to lose Da, and now she would be losing Ma, too. And at Ma's own wish! She clenched her teeth, fighting the tears away, then met her mother's gaze with all the strength and anger she possessed. "How can a mother give away her own children?" she demanded.

46

Ma gripped Frances's shoulders and stared into her eyes. "You heard what I told the judge. It's because I can't provide you with the good home you should have. I can't keep the boys from the streets. I can't fill your stomachs with good food. It's the most painful thing I've ever had to do, Frances, but it's a sacrifice that must be made."

"You don't love us enough to keep us."

"Oh, Frances Mary, don't you realize? It's because I love you so much that I am able to send you away!"

Frances didn't speak. She didn't move to touch her mother, even though a part of her ached to do it. If you loved someone, you kept that person close. You didn't send someone you cared about away to live among strangers. She couldn't understand her mother's mixed-up thinking. Her entire body ached with shock and confusion, and she clenched her teeth against the pain.

"When must we leave?" practical Megan whispered.

"Now," Ma said, and she knelt to enfold her children.

"Please, Ma, no!" Megan sobbed.

Peg, her small freckled face blotchy from tears, hiccupped with dry sobs and clung tightly to one of Ma's legs. Danny and Mike were pale, pressed shoulder to shoulder for support, just the way they had been after Da had died. This was like another death, Frances thought, only she felt as if she were the one who had died. All that was left of her was a hard, cold emptiness that had eaten away everything else inside her.

"I don't want to go away from you!" Petey wrapped his arms tightly around Ma's neck.

"My darling lad, it's for the best," Ma murmured, and Frances could hear Ma's voice tremble with the tears she was holding back.

Ma wiped away Petey's tears and tried to cheer him

47

with a smile, but even when she smiled her face looked lined and exhausted.

"Reverend Brace told me that you'll have wholesome food, and a clean bed of your own, and schooling, and all sorts of fine things, the like of which I could never, ever give you, no matter how hard we work," Ma said.

"But I won't have *you*!" Petey wailed.

"You'll have Frances," Ma told him. She looked up at Frances. "It's a special care this littlest one will be needing," she said, "and it's you I'll be counting on to give it."

Frances just stared back. She wanted to tell her mother how lonely and hurt she was, but the words had frozen in her throat.

"Frances Mary Kelly." Her mother stood to face her, and her voice was firm and strong again. "I want your promise."

Frances nodded, and now her voice matched her mother's in its strength and determination. "I promise," she said. "And I also promise that I'll do my best to be mother to these children in place of the mother who doesn't want them."

"Can't you understand how much it hurts me to see you go?"

"No!" Frances cried. For a moment she wavered. "I can't. I love you, Ma, and I thought you loved me. I can't understand how you could give us away, and I'll never forgive you. Never!"

"Oh!" Ma took a step backward, holding her hands to her cheeks and flinching as though she'd been struck. "Frances Mary, you've never in your life spoken such angry words to me."

Frances just shook her head, unable to say another

48

word. She knew she'd begin to cry uncontrollably if she tried to speak again.

Ma's voice was heavy with sorrow. "You, Frances— you who've been my strength in so many ways, so many times—it's sure I've been that I could count on you, sure that you'd understand."

Frances desperately longed to reach out and hold her mother, but she couldn't. She wouldn't.

Reverend Brace stepped forward and took Peg and Petey by the hand. Peg, her lower lip trembling, tried to tug her hand away, but Petey just stared at Ma, his big blue eyes spilling over with tears. "It's time to go now," Reverend Brace said.

Gently, Ma touched each child, one by one, with her fingertips. "It won't be forever, Danny," she whispered. "We'll someday be together again. Mike, you're a good, brave lad, and you've got a chance now to prove yourself." She smiled. "Remember that I'll always believe in you."

She paused with her hands on Megan's head, as though she were giving a blessing. "My darlin', gentle girl, you're the one who might take this the hardest. Just remember that you come from a strong, sturdy people, who down through the years have had the courage to do what must be done. And Peg—"

Frances could hear the catch in Ma's voice as she stroked Peg's cheek. "Peg, love, there's so much joy in you always spilling out, it will make the going easy. Oh, how I'll miss that happy laughter."

"Ma," Petey whimpered, and Ma bent to hold his face between her hands. "You have nothing to fear, lad. Frances will keep a special watch on you. You're so young, all this will soon be tucked in a far corner of your mind." Frances could barely hear her mother's whisper. "Oh, Petey, don't completely forget your ma!"

Ma rose. "One last kiss before we say good-bye," she said and turned to Frances, holding her tightly. "I know that someday you'll understand and forgive me, love," she murmured. "If I didn't know that, I couldn't bear to see you hurt this way."

Frances's cheek was damp as her mother's tears mingled with her own, but still she didn't speak. Finally Ma let go, her eyes brimming with moisture. Ma's gaze fell on each of her children one more time, then she blew them all a kiss and turned away. Frances watched her mother stride down the hall and desperately fought against the panic that made her want to run screaming after Ma. At the corner of the hall Ma paused, glancing back for just a second before she disappeared from sight.

"Don't leave us, Ma!" Frances whispered. "I want to stay with you! I don't want any part of life in the West!"

5

INSIDE THE CHILDREN'S Aid Society building on Amity Street was a long bench on which the children were told to sit. On a table near the front door was a pile of freshly ironed dresses, shirts, trousers, stockings, and underclothes. Frances could read the note that was pinned on top of the pile: "A donation for the children."

"Please be seated," Reverend Brace said. He smiled reassuringly. "Mrs. Minton will join us in a few minutes, and you'll soon meet the other children who'll make the trip with you."

"Will you go to the West with us?" Peg asked, her voice wobbling. She clung to his hand.

Mr. Brace gently removed her hand from his and patted it. "No," he said. "I'm needed here in New York. But you'll have two fine people who'll take care of you during your trip. Mr. Andrew MacNair is my scout. It's his job to find good farm families who will adopt you.

And helping him on this trip is Mrs. Katherine Banks, who runs a general store in the town of St. Joseph."

"St. Joseph is a town?" Danny blurted out in surprise.

"In Missouri," Mr. Brace answered. "That's your destination."

Frances had a question of her own. "Please, Reverend Brace," she said, "can you tell me about my friend, Mara Robi?"

"Of course," he said and looked down the hall. "Mrs. Minton should be here at any moment. If you don't mind waiting alone, I'll go to my office and check with someone who will know exactly how Mara is doing."

The children squeezed together on the bench. No one seemed to feel like talking. Next to the bench was an open door to an office, and Frances could easily hear the conversation between a man and two women inside the room.

"I brought some clothes I collected for the poor, dear orphans," a woman announced.

"Thank you, Mrs. Marsh." This voice belonged to a younger woman.

"How many boys and how many girls will you take on this trip, Mr. MacNair?" Mrs. Marsh asked.

"I haven't made a tally yet," the man said. "But I think we'll have more boys than girls, which is good. It's always easier to place boys, because boys can help with the outdoor farm chores. Some families will even take two children from a family if they're boys."

Frances took a quick breath. She had heard her mother speak of *homes*, but she had been so upset and distracted that she hadn't realized what Ma had meant. They were going to be separated!

Frances knew that Megan, Mike, and Danny had understood, too. Megan gave a little whimper and shivered as she nuzzled closer to her sister.

"We'll stick together, you and me, huh, Mike?" Frances heard Danny whisper, and she sighed at the desperate hope in his voice.

"What ages are the children?" the woman asked.

"All ages," Mr. MacNair said, "up to our top age limit of fourteen."

A frantic jumble of thoughts tossed through Frances's head. What was she going to do? She had promised to take special care of Petey. She had to keep Petey with her. She raised a hand and fingered her long hair. Ma had loved that hair, which was just the color of her mother's.

After the sound of shuffling papers and a squeaking chair, Mr. MacNair said, "Let's see if Charles has returned. I have some questions to ask him."

The women and man left the office, smiling at the children as they passed them. After a quick glance, Frances looked away. She hoped they hadn't noticed her. She kept a sharp watch. As soon as they had disappeared into a room near the end of the hallway, Frances jumped to her feet. She pulled her hand away from Petey, then pried off his fingers as he clutched at her skirt.

"Listen to me!" she whispered, and they all did, recognizing the urgency in her voice. "I'm going outside for just a few minutes. When I come back I'll look different, and I want all of you to call me Frankie. Frances is all right, if you forget, because that can be a boy's name, too. But whatever you do, don't call me Frances *Mary*!"

"But, what—?" Peg began, as she squirmed on the bench.

"Peg!" Frances interrupted. "Pay attention. This is important. I'm going to dress like a boy. You must remember. I'll be Frankie, your *brother*, not your sister!"

Megan's eyes were wide. "You can't do that!" she said.

"For a little while I can. Just for a while."

"Why?" Danny asked.

"So Petey and I can stay together," Frances said. "If it's boys to do the chores that those farm families are wanting, then it's a boy I'll become." Frances paused and added, "Will you remember my new name, Petey?"

His eyes suddenly sparkled with mischief. "Is this a game?"

"No. It's not a game," Frances said. "You must not forget." She turned to the others. "Will all of you remember?"

Megan, Peg, and Danny nodded, but Mike laughed. "Just how are you going to look like a boy, with that long hair and those skirts?"

"Do you still have your pocketknife?"

"Yes."

"Then give it to me quickly," Frances said. With the knife in her hand, she ran to the table of clothing and snatched up a boy's cotton shirt and trousers. Then she ran out the door and around the corner of the building to the alley. Dropping the clothing to the ground, Frances quickly opened the knife, grabbed a hank of her long hair, then shuddered at the sound of the metal blade raggedly cutting through the thick, resistant mass.

In a few minutes Frances, dressed in boys' clothes, hair cropped short, raced back into the building. She stopped short when she saw the plump, gray-haired woman who stood in front of the bench and held her breath, waiting to see how the woman would react to her. Petey and Peg were sniffling, and Megan was pale, her eyes dark and frightened. Her brothers and sisters stared with astonishment as Frances quickly slid next to them on the bench.

"Sorry, ma'am," Frances said, trying to keep her voice from trembling. "I—uh—had to go outside."

"It's all right," the woman said. She studied a small sheet of paper, then looked up and smiled at Megan. "You must be Frances Mary, dear. Reverend Brace told me to inform you that your friend, Mara, is still in the hospital, but she is recovering nicely."

Megan quickly glanced at her sister. Frances's joy and relief about Mara were dampened by fear that her disguise would be found out. Quickly she stammered, "*I'm* Francis, and it's not Mary, it's—uh—Martin. But forget the 'Martin' part. Just call me Frankie."

Mrs. Minton stared hard at the paper. "My, my," she said. "The handwriting doesn't look that hard to read."

Mike gave Frances a hard clip on the shoulder, and she winced. "She thinks you look like a girl, Frankie. Huh! Where are your pretty curls?"

Frances landed a sock on Mike's arm before he could lean out of the way, and Mrs. Minton quickly said, "Don't do that, boys! You can't behave like that around here!"

"I don't look like a girl!" Frances muttered as fiercely as she could.

"Of course you don't," Mrs. Minton said. "Somewhere there was a mistake in this list of names, and it's certainly not your fault."

Peg stood, her chin held high. "I am Margaret Ann Kelly," she announced proudly, "no matter what that paper says, but everybody calls me 'Peg.'"

Mrs. Minton went on to meet the other Kelly children, one by one, then smoothed the long white apron that covered her dark cotton dress. "I know this is a difficult experience for you children, so I'll try to make it easier by explaining what we're going to do."

Peg sniffled, and Mrs. Minton said, "Don't cry, dear. Think about the pretty new dress you'll soon be wearing." She smiled and patted Peg's shoulder, handing her a small, lacy handkerchief before she continued. "To begin with, my name is Mrs. Minton. I'm going to see that each of you has a nice warm bath. I'll expect you boys to use plenty of soap on your hair, too, and I'll help the girls." She stared for a moment at Frances's hair. "I'm very good at trimming hair. You'll want to start your journey with a nice tidy haircut, won't you?"

"Yes, ma'am," Frances stuttered. A bath? Oh, no! She'd be discovered before they even left New York! She felt a hot blush creep over her neck and face, and she ducked her head. Mike snickered so softly that only Frances could hear it, and she answered by poking her elbow into his ribs.

They were led to the bathing rooms for boys and for girls. Frances hesitated at the door to the boys' room, but Mike shoved her, and she stumbled inside to find the room empty.

"The other children have already bathed," Mrs. Minton said. "There's plenty of hot water in the tub, and be sure to wash well behind your ears. You'll find clothes and shoes in all sizes on the shelves along the far wall. If you want any help, just call."

"We won't need any help!" Frances said quickly.

"Then I'll lend a hand to the girls. As soon as you've dressed, just open the door, and I'll return," Mrs. Minton said. She shut the door behind her as she left.

"Being as we're all boys, shouldn't we all get into the tub together?" Mike asked with a grin.

"Unless you'd like another bloody nose, which I could well give you, you'll sit with Danny and Petey on that bench, backs to the tub, until I've finished," Frances said with such determination that Mike put a quick stop to his teasing.

After the baths, the children searched through the

clothing to find clothes and shoes or boots that fit. Petey, Danny, Mike, and Frances were finally outfitted in dark woolen pants and jackets, collarless cotton shirts buttoned under their chins, dark stockings, and high, side-buttoned boots. Because Petey was so young, his shirt had a collar and a wide, navy-blue bow. They opened the door, and Mrs. Minton returned to comb and trim their hair. When she was finished, she lined them up and beamed at them.

"You look wonderful." she said. "Now come and see your lovely sisters."

Frances and the boys followed her into the next room where Peg and Megan were perched on chairs. "Look at me!" Peg cried. "Look at my beautiful blue dress!"

Frances caught Peg in her arms. "I once saw a girl wearing a coat that was this very shade of blue," she said. "You're every bit as beautiful as she was."

She turned to Megan. "And you're a real beauty in that dark red dress, Megan." Frances sadly wondered how she would have looked wearing a proper high-waisted dress and pantalets, with a ribbon tying back her hair.

But Megan blushed and ducked her head. "You don't have to say that, Fr-Frankie. You know I've always been plain."

"Well, you're not plain now," Frances said firmly. She took Megan's hand and pulled her to her feet. "I just noticed—your eyes are as big and blue as Petey's."

Mrs. Minton patted Megan's shoulder. "Wait right here, children. I'll be back in just a minute."

As she left the room Peg said proudly, "I have new shoes."

Petey's mouth curled down abruptly. "I don't like

57

shoes," he complained. "My toes can't wiggle, and my feet can't breathe."

Mike picked Petey up and laughed. "Feet don't breathe! Besides, my fine lad, you'd better get used to shoes, because where you're going everybody wears shoes."

Petey began to whimper. "I don't want shoes. I want Ma!"

Peg's lower lip jutted out. "It's Mike's fault that we're here."

Stricken, Mike stared at Peg, but Danny shoved her, almost knocking her off-balance. "Don't ever say that again!" he shouted.

Megan stepped forward, holding Peg protectively. "Leave her alone, Danny! She's upset."

"I'll not have her blaming Mike! And don't you, either!"

"Stop yelling at me!" Peg demanded.

"I'm not yelling!"

"You are so!" Megan said.

"Stop it, all of you," Frances said. "It's not Mike's fault that we're here, and I'll not hear another word of blame from a one of us." She met the gaze of each of them in turn. "We'll have to stick together, come what may, and that's the all of it."

For a moment there was silence. Then Danny murmured, "You sounded just like Ma."

Frances gulped back the sob that rose in her throat. Without a word Megan reached for her sister's hand, and Frances gratefully took it.

Mrs. Minton returned and led them all to a large room in which children of all ages were gathered around a tall young woman with sandy hair, green eyes, and a smattering of freckles across her nose. She was dressed in a deep brown, tailored traveling dress trimmed in rows of black braid.

Most of the children ignored the Kellys, but a little girl of about four, the ends of her pale, wispy hair flying about her face, took her thumb from her mouth and said to Peg, "Are you going with me?"

"Where are you going?" Peg asked.

"I'm going to the West with her, with Katherine." She pointed to the tall woman.

"We're going west, too," Peg said.

Satisfied, the little girl nodded. "A mother and father will adopt me. Katherine said they would."

"What's *adopt* mean?" Peg asked her.

The little girl thought for a moment, then said, "It means what Katherine said. I will still be Clara, but I will have a mother." She looked at Peg. "Do you have a mother?"

A tear began to roll down Peg's cheek as she nodded vigorously.

"Let's find some string. Have you ever played cat's cradle?" Mrs. Minton asked. She took both little girls by the hand and briskly walked away.

Frances counted the children in the room. Twenty-eight, most of them boys, many of them older and taller than she.

One of the older boys made his way through the group and clapped Mike on the shoulder.

"Jim!" Mike said. "So you're going west, too."

Jim shrugged. "I figured the West couldn't be worse and might be a lot better than what I had."

"What you had? You didn't have anything." Mike grinned, and Jim grinned back.

"All the children are here now, Katherine," Mrs. Minton shouted over the loud chatter, laughter, shrieks, and occasional sobs that filled the room.

Peg ran back to join her family, a circle of string

59

dangling from her hand. She began to loop her fingers through the string, her face somber with concentration on the game. "Look!" she said, holding up the string, woven into the shape of a cradle, to Megan. "You do it!"

The woman Clara had called Katherine stepped to the side of the room and clapped her hands for attention. As soon as everyone had turned her way, she said, "Children, my name is Katherine Banks. I'm going to be with you on your trip to St. Joseph, Missouri.

"We'll be leaving soon for the train station, and our ride will take a number of days. When we get to St. Joseph, many families will come to meet us. We'll introduce you to them, and they'll choose you to come and live with them."

Voices called out. "What if they don't like us?" "What if nobody wants us?"

In the silence, as the children waited for the answer, Frances heard Megan's long, shuddering sigh.

"Believe me, they'll want you," Katherine said. "They're eagerly waiting for you to arrive."

Katherine's voice was cheerful, but Frances doubted the words. Who would want children whose own mother didn't want them? She shivered.

One of the taller boys asked, "But what if we don't like the people who want us?"

Again the room was very quiet as Katherine answered, "This choice will be yours, too. We'd never make you go with a family if you didn't want to."

"We aren't in much of a spot to object—are we, now?" Jim said with a laugh. Some of the older boys joined in the laughter, shoving at one another and hooting, trying to cover their fears, Frances knew.

Katherine held up her hands until everyone was quiet again. "When you're placed with a family you'll be treated like kin. You'll be expected to do chores along with the rest of the family, but you'll also get schooling and a warm, comfortable bed of your own, and plenty of good food." She smiled, and her voice grew even warmer. "And oh, how you'll love the fresh vegetables and fruit and meat, and the warm milk from the cows, and the big open sky, and the places to run and play. In the summer the fields are high with grass and wildflowers. In the winter the snow covers the land as far as you can see, but you'll go sledding and build snowmen, and maybe even take sleigh rides."

All the children began to murmur to one another.

Frances scowled as she thought. This was a scene she couldn't picture. Who would want strange children from the New York streets to take care of along with their own? And why should they give them all these fine things? Katherine's telling sounded very much the way Ma and Da must have imagined America to be—which turned out to be far from the truth for them.

Peg, at seven years much shorter than many of the other children, suddenly stood on tiptoe and shouted over the hubbub, "You said we'd each have a bed, miss. But I don't want my own bed. A bed would be lonely without all my brothers and sisters in it. I want to be with them."

"Dear child . . ." Katherine said, and for a moment she looked distressed. "Mr. MacNair will do his best to place you and your brothers and sisters near one another, so you can stay in touch." She added quietly, "But I can't even promise you that."

Before anyone could ask another question, a tall gentleman entered the room and strode with long steps to join Katherine. His smiling face was deeply tanned, almost the same color as his sun-bleached brown hair. The dark gray material in his suit coat strained across his broad shoulders, and the stiff, high collar of his white shirt seemed almost out of place. *He's an out-of-doors man, like Da was,* Frances thought. *And he's almost as handsome as Da.* Frances was surprised when her cheeks suddenly turned warm, and she ducked her head so that no one could see her blush.

The man introduced himself as Mr. Brace's scout, Andrew MacNair, and reassured the children that they'd be placed in good homes.

From then on, events happened so quickly that Frances had little time to think about them. First, Andrew and Katherine took the children by horse-drawn car to the noisy, reeking docks, where they were led aboard a paddle wheeler, which began the trip up the Hudson River to Albany.

Frances found herself shoved by the crowd of excited children against the rail around the boat's lower deck, where she watched the New York skyline recede into the distance. New York City had been the only home she'd ever known, and she wondered if she would ever see it again. She thought about the room in which they had lived, and she could picture Ma, sewing in the chair near the small window, leaning into its meager light. She tried next to picture the room of her dreams, with Ma laughing and swirling the skirts of her beautiful green coat, but the image wouldn't come. It had abandoned her, just as Ma had.

Frances gripped the rail, tears burning her eyes. "Good-bye, Ma," she whispered. "Good-bye."

6

THE TRAIN STATION at Albany was a noisy, busy place, with passengers and visitors, bustling with armloads of parcels and baggage, crowding the platform and talking loudly to be heard as they waited for the train to arrive. But a hush fell over the platform as a huge, silver-and-black monster, trimmed in red and brass, a high, conical stack over its gleaming eye, huffed and creaked into the station.

As soon as they had been given permission, the children climbed aboard one of the railcars near the end of the train, following Andrew. "Wait, Mike!" Frances called, but Mike scrambled aboard, Danny right behind him. Mike had to be tugged back by Andrew's strong hand as he leaned far out one of the windows to reach a hand to Petey.

"Only through the door!" Andrew said sternly.

Breathlessly Frances boosted Petey up the steps, making sure that Peg and Megan were right behind him.

She stopped just inside the door. On each side of a narrow aisle were rows of wooden seats that faced forward. Each was wide enough for two adults, so three—or even four—children could squeeze together easily. From the ceiling at the center of the car hung a whale-oil lamp. Wide sash windows were open to catch the breeze, but previous breezes apparently had carried with them plenty of cinder dust from the smokestack. A fine film of grit covered the seats and floors. Narrow wooden racks, where Andrew was now busy stowing parcels, hung above the seats.

The children were not the only passengers in this car. A plump woman cringed and pulled her skirt from the aisles each time one of the children passed by her seat. With her was a gentleman whose gray sideburns swept almost to his chin. He tapped his silver-headed cane on the floor and muttered loudly to his wife, "Not another batch of orphans! I've said it before, they're all young criminals and should be kept in New York City."

Danny, with a flare of quick temper that matched his red hair, bristled, but Katherine held his arm. "Mr. Crandon will change his mind when he discovers what fine young people you are," she murmured.

Frances looked up at her gratefully. Maybe she would like Katherine Banks. At least Katherine seemed to be on the children's side.

"Do you know Mr. Crandon?" Danny asked.

"Amos Crandon is an important businessman in St. Joseph," Katherine answered. "He's well respected and most successful."

"But he doesn't like us already," Danny murmured. "Maybe nobody will."

Frances shivered as Danny put her fears into words. What if nobody wanted them? What would happen to

64

them then? She quickly shoved the terrifying thought away.

"You can be sure that someone will like you," Katherine said. She patted Danny's shoulder and left to find seats for the other children.

A few of the passengers smiled at the children and stopped to ask Katherine where they were going. A young woman wearing an elegant rose dress with a matching jacket, who had paused to chat, yelped and pulled Clara out from under her wide hoopskirt.

"But I never in my life seen anything like that!" Clara exclaimed loudly. "And there's ruffles all the way from her ankles to her knees!"

The woman, blushing furiously, handed Clara over to Katherine, who held her on her lap. Frances, remembering she was supposed to be a boy and would get into trouble for snickering, turned away quickly and tried not to laugh.

"All aboard!" voices yelled.

"Over here, Abby!"

"Come on, Hal!"

"Jim, where are you?"

The children scrambled onto the benches. Frances slipped into a seat next to a window and put an arm around Petey, who yawned and snuggled against her.

Within a few minutes they'd begin their journey. This wasn't just her first train ride. It was the start of a new life. Frances's stomach was tight with fear, but as she looked around the car, she shivered with excitement. The sight of all these curious people headed west on the very same train as Frances Mary Kelly, disguised as a boy, made her begin to believe anything could happen. At the thought of her disguise and her promise to Ma, Frances's feelings became even more of a jumble. Guiltily, she wondered why Ma couldn't share the new life that she and her brothers and sisters were going to have. But her mother had chosen to send them away while she stayed behind. Resentment swept away Frances's guilt. "Ma! Oh, Ma!" she whispered. "How could you do this to us?" If only she could sneak off somewhere, put down her head, and cry.

She noticed Mike glance at her, so she took a deep breath and pushed her feelings away. She was the eldest. She was in charge. She had to be the responsible, strong one.

Without warning, the train started up with a series of jerks and jounces that threw Frances against the back of the seat, and she let out a yelp.

The train picked up speed and rattled forward, quickly leaving the station and the city of Albany behind. Frances soon became used to the rhythmic swaying of the car and stared out the window, entranced by the countryside. The tidy, white-painted houses were so different from the crowded, dark brick ones of New York. These houses were trimmed with blue or green shutters and next to them were planted neat, square gardens bursting with gold and russet marigolds and deep green vegetables in straight rows. "Cabbages!" Frances shouted as she recognized one of the vegetables.

No one seemed to hear her. All the children were racing back and forth across the aisle, peering out the windows and shouting.

"Apples! Look at the apples!"

"Over here! See the woolies!"

"Horses! With men on their backs!"

"I want to see the horses!" Petey bounced up and down with excitement. "I want to ride on a horse!"

"Look at the dogs with the funny noses!" one of the

younger children shouted, and most of the children rushed to the left side of the car.

One of the older boys laughed. "Those ain't dogs! They're pigs! I seen pigs brought in down at the docks."

Frances waved at a woman who had looked up from her hoeing. The woman raised her hand and waved back before she bent once more to her chore. Frances smiled and was filled with relief. Perhaps Katherine had been telling the truth. Was this the kind of friendship she would find in the West? For the first time she felt encouraged.

"Did you see?" Frances asked Petey. "She waved at us! And look—over on the hill—look at the cows."

"Cows?" There was another rush, this time to the right side of the train.

"But what does a cow *do*?" Peg asked.

"She gives milk," Frances answered.

Peg giggled and said to Megan, "Frances said a cow gives us milk! Everybody knows that it's Mr. Zeit with his milk cart who gives us milk."

Peg's lower lip turned out as her statement was met with a roar of laughter. But Katherine scooped her up and held her on her lap. "In a few minutes the train will make a stop for wood and water. Andrew will buy some fresh milk for you then. Will you like that?"

"Oh, yes!" Peg forgot the laughter and snuggled against Katherine.

Petey spoke up. "Do you have a husband?" he asked Katherine. "Why didn't you bring him with you?"

"My husband, John, died three years ago," Katherine said.

"Don't you have any children?" Petey asked, but Frances quickly hushed him.

"I'm sorry," she murmured.

"It's all right," Katherine said and reached over to pat

Petey's knee. "I wish we had had some children. It's just not the way things worked out."

"Do you have a farm?" Peg asked.

"Not a farm, a general store, where all the farmers for miles and miles around come to buy supplies. John and I opened the store, and I've kept it up and made it grow." She nuzzled the back of Peg's neck, making her giggle. "What would you like to buy in my store? A new hair ribbon? A sack of flour? A paper twist filled with sugar?"

Andrew sat on the bench next to Frances and said, "Katherine has left the store to her assistant to run, because I asked for her help. I'm lucky to have her."

Katherine smiled at Andrew so warmly that Frances felt a stab of jealousy. *Why should I feel this way?* she asked herself. All she understood was that she liked having Andrew squeezed on the bench so close that she could feel the warmth of his arm against hers. Frances's face began to burn, and she turned toward the window, letting the cold breeze sting her skin.

"We're slowing down!" someone yelled, and the children rushed to fill any available window.

"Everyone stay put," Andrew announced. "This will be a quick stop, and I'm not about to leave one of you behind."

It didn't take long for the men at the station to load stacks of wood on the open car behind the engine and to swing a pipe down from a large tank to fill the boiler with water. Andrew emerged from the building with a covered pail and dashed to the steps just as the train began to move.

Bread and cheese were handed around to the children, and they took turns drinking the warm milk from two metal cups which Andrew produced.

68

As the train rushed on, the children shouted out at each new sight. By evening heads were nodding, some of the shrillest voices had quieted, and many of the children had fallen asleep. Those who were awake sat in the aisle or leaned against the benches, listening to the tales told by a young army officer and the gentleman who was seated next to him.

"You were really attacked by Indians?" Frances gasped as the gentleman finished speaking.

"Twice," he said.

The army officer smiled. "Have you ever heard of the Overland Stage Line?"

There was silence. Some of the children shook their heads. But Mike spoke up. "Stagecoaches, like in the dime novels!"

The officer laughed. "This is Mr. Ben Holladay, who has been called by some the 'Stagecoach King,' and I am Captain Joshua Taylor of the United States Army."

"Don't you carry a gun?" Mike asked.

"When I'm traveling I keep it in my satchel."

"Are you going back to the West?" Mike asked.

"Mr. Holladay is going to St. Louis, and I'm being sent to Fort Leavenworth in Kansas," the captain said.

"To fight Indians?" Danny asked, his eyes wide.

"No," Captain Taylor said, "but I'll tell you a story about the first time I fought Indians."

Frances hadn't even noticed when the conductor had lit the lantern in their railcar. Now she was surprised to find the train stopping at another station. Its platform was well lit with a number of whale-oil lanterns.

"Where are we?" Frances asked.

"In Buffalo," Andrew said.

"Buffalos?" Danny's voice was awed. "Are we in the West then?"

"Not yet," Andrew told him. "We're still in the state of New York. We've got a long ride ahead of us."

When the train stopped, some of the adult passengers walked up and down the aisle for exercise. A few got off the train. Two women opened a hamper and brought out a meal, which they ate.

Frances took her seat and stared from the window. People milled about the train. Women in full skirts and warm capes and men bundled into greatcoats with scarves around their necks to shield against the cold night air stood next to trunks and traveling cases. Then Frances noticed a black man being led past the train by two men who carried guns with long black barrels. Flickers of light sparked from the wide metal cuffs that dug into the man's wrists and were attached to the chains one captor was holding.

"Oh, no!" Frances cried, jumping to her feet. "What are they doing to that poor man?"

Captain Taylor joined her at the window. "The man must be a slave," he said. "He probably tried to run away and is being returned to his owner. Do you know what a slave is?"

The slave's shoulders slumped as though every hope had been squeezed from his body. Frances ached for him. "Yes," she whispered. "I know. I wish he had escaped. This is a Free State. He should have got away."

"It wouldn't have helped," Captain Taylor said. "A few years ago Congress passed the Fugitive Slave Act, which means that officials and citizens of Free States are required to aid in capturing runaway slaves and restoring them to their rightful owners."

"That's not fair!" Frances blurted out.

"But it's the law, son," the captain said. "As good citizens we must uphold the law."

"Those men didn't look like good citizens to me."

Nearby a woman commented loudly, "They probably weren't, not if they were bounty hunters."

"What are bounty hunters?" Frances asked.

"They're men who make a living hunting runaway slaves," the captain said.

The woman sniffed. "It doesn't seem right to me that those dreadful men can go into Free States chasing down slaves. Two of those bounty hunters once pushed their way onto our place in Ohio, and my husband had to run them off with a shotgun. Like to scared me to death."

The train started up in its usual bumping fashion. It was late and dark, with only the dim light from the swinging lantern casting wild, moving shadows across the car. As Frances stared out at the landscape, she could see clustered lights of houses that winked through the night. Then the lights became more scattered, until finally there was nothing outside the train but a black, empty world without moonlight or stars.

Frances shifted under the weight of Petey's head on her lap and leaned against the wooden frame of the window, closing her eyes. Megan sniffled beside her, and she reached over to take her hand.

"I keep thinking about what Andrew said," Megan whispered, "about how people don't take all the children in a family. We're going to be sent to different homes. It frightens me. Does it frighten you, too?"

"Yes," Frances said, keeping her voice low. "It does."

"I don't want to think about being parted from you," Megan said. "We've always been together."

Frances squeezed Megan's hand. "Maybe we won't be parted. Maybe someone will say, 'We want all those fine Kelly children!' And they'll take us to their house—a big white house with green—no, blue—shutters, and they'll have a horse for Petey to ride and—"

Megan interrupted. "None of your dreams now, Frances. Dreams are just pretending, and you know they don't come true."

"I wish this one could." Frances groaned. "Oh, if only Ma hadn't—"

But Megan interrupted, her voice breaking. "Please don't talk about Ma now. I miss her too much."

They were silent for a few minutes, and soon Megan fell asleep, her head resting heavily on Frances's shoulder. One of the smaller children in the car was crying, and Frances could hear Katherine's low, comforting murmur. Before long the only sounds in the car were the creaks and groans of the wooden seats and the clatter of iron wheels against the rails, all of which flowed into a steady rhythm. Soon Frances was sound asleep.

7

"WAKE UP, FRANKIE. I want to go home."

Frances awoke stiff and tired as Petey buried his face in her neck, whimpering, "I want Ma!"

"I want Ma, too! Are we ever going to see Ma again?" Peg wailed.

"There, now," Frances soothed, "of course we are." But she kept her eyes downcast, unable to meet theirs. How could she tell them this when she didn't believe it herself? Every turn of the train's wheels took them farther and farther away from Ma. Frances tried to smile, to bolster their spirits, because she was in charge. The others mustn't know that she felt like crying, too.

Frances looked up, feeling Megan's appraising eyes upon her.

Megan brushed back her long, dark hair and whispered, "What will happen to us, Frankie?"

"Why—we'll find good homes. We'll have new families and good food and warm beds," Frances parroted. She reached across Petey and gripped her sister's hand. "Oh, Megan," she whispered, "I honestly don't know what will happen."

One of the younger boys fell into the aisle and let out a yell. At the sound of it another child began to cry.

"Can't someone shut those urchins up!" Mr. Crandon bellowed as the train lurched into motion.

"They're only children," a woman snapped at him.

Mr. Crandon puffed up like a pigeon guarding the only crumb of bread. "Madam, we are entitled to as much peace and quiet as this railroad company can provide."

"I'm sorry." Andrew raised his voice over the din. "We'll feed the children at the next stop, and I can guarantee that will help the situation."

"If you can't control them—" Mr. Crandon began.

But Mike suddenly jumped into the aisle and shouted to the older children, "Hey there, chums! How about a bit of music?" He cupped his hands together and held them against his lips, creating a lively, nasal music as he hummed, and to the music he danced a few wild steps of a jig.

The children who had been crying stopped to stare, then broke into laughter as Mike leaped to click his heels together, lost his balance, and sprawled in the aisle.

Frances saw the twinkle in Mike's eyes and knew he had taken the fall on purpose.

"More! More!" Petey shouted.

So Mike pranced and danced with his odd music, and when some of the older children recognized a tune, they joined in, singing the words. Frances knew "The Irish Washerwoman" and "Old Dog Tray," and when Mike began "Oh! Susanna," some of the adults on the car began to sing, too, Captain Taylor's deep baritone as loud as Andrew's.

Suddenly, with a jolt that tossed Mike sideways onto Katherine's lap, the train shook and rattled to a screeching stop.

"Good work," Katherine murmured to Mike as she helped him regain his balance.

Captain Taylor stretched forward to shake Mike's hand and said, "A wise choice of action, son."

Frances was proud of Mike. He'd been able to make them all forget their aches and fears. Ma would have been proud of Mike, too, if she could have seen him.

Her thoughts were interrupted by the frantic cry of "Fire!"

The conductor threw open the door of the passenger car. "Sparks from the train set a brushfire!" he shouted. "All able-bodied males are needed to help put it out!"

"Come on!" Mike grabbed Frances's arm and tugged her into the aisle. " 'All able-bodied males,' " he wickedly muttered under his breath. "That means you, too!"

"Don't be frightened, boys." Andrew stopped Frances with a firm grip on her shoulder and handed her a wet feed sack as she leapt from the railroad car. "It's not uncommon for sparks to set small brushfires. Just take this sack and join the others."

Deep orange and scarlet flames crawled and crackled through the burning grass, and yellow smoke rose in choking clouds.

Most of the men and boys had poured from the train, grabbed the wet sacks, and were slapping them at the smoldering grass. Frances, hands shaking with terror, copied their actions. Working hard, slamming her dripping sack on the flames, dipping it over and over into the bucket and slamming it again, she was soon absorbed in beating back the low spurts of flame.

"Look out! You're on fire!"

Frances jumped, but it was Amos Crandon Mike meant.

Mr. Crandon froze with fear as the back of his shirt-tail burst into flame.

"Your shirt, man! Pull it off!" Andrew shouted and began to run toward Mr. Crandon.

But Mike was faster. He dove toward the backs of Mr. Crandon's knees. Mr. Crandon bent in two and fell over Mike, sitting down hard. Mike scrambled on top of the man and pushed him on his back, rolling him over and flinging himself across him.

Mike sat up and examined the scorched shirt. "Fire's out," he announced happily.

Mr. Crandon angrily sputtered, "How dare you push me to the ground? You ought to be whipped!"

Frances wanted to defend Mike but was too furious to do anything but sputter. She was glad that Andrew seemed as surprised as Mike by Mr. Crandon's outburst. She caught her breath as Andrew spoke up: "Your shirt was on fire. Mike put it out and kept you from getting burned."

Mr. Crandon glared at Andrew. He brushed the dirt from his clothes and, muttering to himself, unaware that two large spots of very pink skin were showing through holes in his trousers, stomped to the train.

Andrew patted Mike's shoulder, and Frances said, "You did the right thing, Mike." But it wasn't at Mike that she was looking. Andrew was a fine man, a really good and kind man like Da. Oh, how Frances yearned to be called Frances Mary again!

"On board, everybody," the conductor yelled as he

collected the dirty, charred feed sacks. "Fire's out. Get back on board so we can get under way."

"After this train ride is over," Mike muttered to Frances as they climbed the steps to their car, "I hope I'll never see ol' Crandon again!"

The train rattled its way west, stopping every twenty-five miles or so for water and wood. Frances gazed dreamily out over the open hills, the dim forests, the tidy squares of farmland, and the rippling, gray-gold grasslands. The train crossed trestles and bridges and passed towns that all began to look alike to Frances. Occasionally she'd wonder if this type of farm or that kind of house would be like the one where she'd live. Sometimes she'd just sit back, her arm around Petey, and let herself be rocked by the steady rhythm of the rackety wheels that clattered over and over, "New life, new life, new life."

"But I don't want a new life," Frances murmured to herself.

"Mike and I are going to be together," Danny came to tell Frances.

Terror showed in his eyes though, and Frances said what she knew he wanted to hear: "There's a very good chance you will be."

"The people who adopt the children—are most of them kind, do you think?" Megan whispered so softly that Frances could hardly hear her.

"I'm sure they are," Frances said. "Why else would they come?"

"That's a good question," Mike said, "and I haven't found an answer to it yet. Just why would anyone want us?"

Frances put on a brave face and even managed a

laugh. "Because we're a fine lot, we are, and those who get us will be lucky! That's why!"

For the moment they were content, but Frances's heart ached as she realized her words meant nothing. If she was saying only what they wanted to hear, was that what Katherine and Andrew were doing, too?

Days became nights, and nights broke into early day-lights with passengers so stiff they grimaced as they stretched their legs and rubbed their arms and necks. The children and the other passengers dozed, ate, and talked. Occasionally conversation in the car grew lively, especially when the topic turned to politics and the pros and cons of slavery. Frances listened and soaked up the words when someone echoed what Da had told her.

The children changed to another train in the massive Chicago railroad station. This one would take them to the Mississippi River, where they'd cross over, heading toward Hannibal, Missouri.

Missouri! Frances would be glad to see the long train ride end, but her hands grew damp and she found it hard to breathe whenever she thought about what might await her and her brothers and sisters in St. Joseph.

The car in which they rode southwest toward Hanni-bal looked much the same as the first one. Outside the city, even the farms and houses looked like those they had seen for so many days, and most of the passengers on their car were the same. Frances knew that everyone was as exhausted as she was, even the adults. She re-membered the flounces and parasols and grand top hats the ladies and gentlemen wore when they got on the first train in Albany. Now their once-elegant suit coats and wide, bustled dresses were wilted and dusty.

When Petey put his mouth to Frances's ear and whispered loudly, "Some of the people stink," Frances could only nod in agreement.

Mike and another boy got into a shoving match in the aisle, and Frances found herself scolding Mike with an overly sharp tongue. Mike snapped back, rudely sticking out his tongue, and it was all she could do not to slap him.

Arguments exploded among all the children as quickly and often as sparks from a burning, sap-filled log. Tousled and rumpled, Peg and Danny poked at each other unmercifully, and Petey cried over every little thing. Even Megan, who was usually gentle and even-tempered, huddled into a miserable heap next to the window.

Early one evening they reached the broad Mississippi River, which they would cross by steamboat. Standing with the others who clustered at the rail of the big paddle wheeler, Frances begged, "Please, could we stay outside to watch?"

"It's cold and damp," Katherine said. She touched Frances's cheek. "You'll be soaked by the mist rising from the water."

"We don't mind," Frances said. "It's such a big river, and so many, many boats!"

Jim stepped up beside her. "Please?" he echoed. "We want to see it all!"

Katherine laughingly agreed, but while most of the children ran up and down the deck, Jim pointed out some of the types of boats to Frances.

"I'm going to work on a boat," he said. "Maybe one of those big steamboats with twin stacks." His voice filled with yearning as he added, "Maybe a captain and his wife will adopt me."

He continued to lean on the rail, eagerly studying the heavy river traffic. But Frances soon lost interest in the

79

boats and kept an eye on the Missouri shore ahead, watching it appear from the mists as they grew nearer.

When they arrived in Hannibal, Missouri, many passengers left to journey to St. Louis, and other passengers joined them on a third train.

We're actually in Missouri, Frances thought, and she couldn't eat a bite of the food that Andrew had brought on board for their supper.

Although Danny gobbled down his meal, Mike's appetite seemed to have disappeared, too. Frances glanced at Mike just as he looked up at her, and she knew that he shared her terror of what they might have to face when they reached St. Joseph.

"Frances," he said, then quickly corrected himself. "Frankie, I'm sorry about all this. I know that being sent west has been awful hard on you, what with you and Ma so close."

Frances quickly shook her head. "We don't have to talk about it."

"But I want to, because it's my fault that all the rest of you are here, and I'm sorry I did this to you."

"Oh, Mike." Frances reached out to touch her brother's hand. "I don't blame you." She tried to make her voice light. "Look at it this way. You kept telling me I'd like living in the West. Now I'll have a chance to find out."

But Mike didn't respond to her attempt at humor. "This is our last time to be together. After we're placed, who knows when we'll see each other again?"

"We may not know when we'll be together again, but I'm sure that we will be. I'll write to you. Will you write back?"

Mike nodded. "Sure. And someday—"

But the train squealed to such a sudden stop that they were thrown off-balance.

"Outlaws!" a woman screamed as a heavily bearded man burst through the door to their car, waving a rifle at the passengers.

Shrieks and yells came from the other cars as men on horseback galloped at each side of the train. One of the men reined in his horse and poked a long gun in through one of the open windows of the children's car.

The bearded man waved a small cloth sack at the passengers. "Sit down right now! All of you! And don't do anything we don't tell you to do," he snapped.

As she dropped back onto the bench, Frances saw Captain Taylor glance at the man on horseback outside the window and back to the outlaw in the aisle. She held her breath, wondering what he would do. But he sat quietly and kept his hand away from his satchel and his gun.

"Everybody pay attention," the outlaw demanded, little drops of spittle glittering on his beard. "Put your money and valuables in this sack." When they were slow to react he yelled, "Now!" and jabbed the end of his rifle at Mr. Crandon's stomach.

"Don't do that!" Mr. Crandon squeaked. "I'll give you all my money! See! Here it is!" He fumbled for a wad of bills held with a gleaming gold money clip and dropped it into the sack.

The outlaw moved up the aisle, thrusting the open sack ahead of him, his nervous eyes darting from one passenger to another. One by one the passengers obeyed as the outlaw eyed them closely. The women even stripped off their rings and bracelets and dropped them into the sack, and some of the men gave up their pocket watches.

As the outlaw came to Katherine she said, "I have no money."

He glanced at her hand. "You have a ring. Take it off."

"Oh, please let me keep it!" Katherine said. Frances was amazed to see tears in her eyes. "It's not of much value, but it means a great deal to me."

The man quickly glanced at the man on horseback, then back at Katherine, and his voice grew even more loud and harsh. "You heard me! Drop it in the sack! Now!"

As Katherine obeyed, the outlaw outside the window called, "Get a move on! We're ready to ride!"

Cautiously, his gun held before him, the bearded outlaw began to back away from the passengers. Suddenly Mike was in the aisle, plowing into the man, and they stumbled together as the cloth bag was almost jerked from the outlaw's hand. Angrily the man regained his balance, giving Mike such a hard clout with his left hand that he knocked him sprawling. Mike bounced off the edge of the nearest seat and landed on the floor of the car, curled facedown, not moving.

Frances gasped and rushed toward Mike as the outlaw jumped from the car. She could hear more yelling and the sound of galloping horses as he and the rest of his gang raced away from the train. The sound of gunshots exploded outside the window, and Captain Taylor shouted, "Got one of them! But just in the shoulder, blast it!"

"Mike! Wake up!" Frances begged as she threw her arms around him. Danny dove in next to her, and in the next minute Andrew and Katherine were beside her, ready to help. But Mike squirmed away from Frances, struggled to his knees, and stood up, one fist clenched against his chest.

Frances scrambled to her feet, too, trying once more to put her arms around her brother. "Oh, Mike! Are you hurt?"

Mike pulled away to face all the other staring passengers. Frances could see him try to smile, but tears filled his eyes.

"I was a copper stealer once." Mike's voice was barely a whisper. "I promised Ma and I promised myself that I would never pick pockets again, but I couldn't let that outlaw take Mrs. Banks's ring, not when it meant so much to her."

He held out his fist and dropped the ring into Katherine's hand.

"Oh!" Katherine gasped. "Oh, Mike!" She held the ring up to stare at it as though she couldn't believe it was really there, and tears came to her eyes, too. Quickly she bent to wrap Mike in a hug.

Around them people murmured, "How did he manage that?" "What did that boy do?"

"There's more," Mike mumbled against Katherine's shoulder. When she stepped back he held out his hand, palm up, and opened his fingers. In it lay a wad of bills. As everyone stared, Mike gave the lot to Andrew. "I couldn't get it all," he apologized, "but maybe those who lost their money could divide this."

"Good, good!" Mr. Crandon stretched to see, then scowled. "What's this! What about me? He didn't retrieve my gold money clip!"

One of the women began to chirp like a frightened bird. "The bag will be almost empty! What if that outlaw notices and comes back?"

Mike shook his head. "He won't notice. I dropped my

book in the bag to give it weight." He managed a shaky grin. "The tales in those novels about brave, daring outlaws are wrong. There wasn't anything grand about that man. He was dirty and fat and smelled like a New York gutter in summer.'"

Katherine put an arm around Mike's shoulders, hugging him again. "You risked your life!" she said. "You shouldn't have done that." As Mike ducked his head Katherine slipped the ring back onto her finger and added quickly, "But oh, Mike, my friend, I thank you with all my heart for retrieving my ring."

Captain Taylor stepped forward to shake Mike's hand. "You exhibited great courage," he said. "I'm proud of you."

Mr. Crandon's booming voice almost drowned out the captain's words. "You all heard that boy. He admitted to being a copper stealer, a common pickpocket!"

"Just a minute, Mr. Crandon!" Katherine said. "This is the boy who saved your life during the fire."

But Mr. Crandon sputtered, "Saved my life? That's debatable! All I know is that he ruined my trousers!"

"You're not being fair to Mike! He risked his life with that outlaw to try to save some of our property."

"He tried to help!" Danny echoed as he stepped in front of Mike.

Mr. Crandon wrinkled his nose as though he'd just smelled something bad. "Granted, the boy thought he was doing right," he said. "I'll give you that much. But don't you see? It simply proves my point. He's never learned the right values."

"That's not true!" Frances exclaimed, but Mr. Crandon ignored her.

"A boy like that should not be allowed in a proper home! And I'll do my best to see to it that he isn't!"

84

"Mr. Crandon—" Andrew began.

But a woman who had boarded the train at Hannibal raised her voice to shout over his. "I agree. Perhaps the boy could be sent back to New York."

Her companion clutched the lapels of her jacket together as though Mike had plans to steal it and stammered, "I think Mr. Crandon should take steps to see this is done. We don't need a New York pickpocket here!"

"No!" Frances could stay quiet no longer. She stepped in front of Mike and faced the surprised passengers.

"In New York," she said, "we worked very hard, but we didn't always have enough to eat. And we didn't have clean, fine clothes like those we're wearing now. And we didn't have our father. Da died last year. Mike was wrong to steal, but he thought he had to so that he could bring home a bit of meat now and then. He tried in his own way to help."

She took a long breath and hurried on before she could lose what little courage she had left. "We're people just like you, who have the same feelings you have."

The woman who earlier had spoken up for the children held out a hand, as though she were reaching for Frances, and said, "Oh, my dear child, it's plain that some of us have forgotten that you had no parents to guide you."

"We have a parent. We have a mother," Frances said, "and she and Da taught us, over and over again, the rules we should follow."

"You have a mother? But where is she?"

Frances held her chin up, willing it to stop trembling. "She sent us west," she said, trying to repeat Ma's words without thinking about them, "because she wanted us to have better lives than she could give us."

85

Without another word the passengers drifted back to their seats. The children, subdued and silent now, sat clustered together on the benches.

Andrew squeezed into the seat next to Frances. "Well spoken, son," he said. "I think you and Mike will do very well for yourselves in the West."

Frances glanced back at Mr. Crandon. She couldn't help being afraid, not just for Mike, but for all of them. Every minute was taking them closer to St. Joseph, to the place she had never seen that might be her home for the rest of her life. What would happen to them then?

8

EARLY IN THE morning, as they approached the town of St. Joseph, Frances wistfully watched Katherine busy herself with brushing and braiding the girls' long hair. From under a seat Katherine pulled a small valise and began extracting fresh hair bows from it as though she were a magician.

Katherine smoothed and straightened dresses, tidied jackets, and made sure that all buttons were buttoned. Frances brushed off her own jacket with trembling fingers.

"You look wonderful," Katherine said. "The people who come to meet you will be impressed."

For a moment the children were quiet, then Danny spoke up. "What if no one comes?"

Katherine laughed, and Andrew seemed surprised. He motioned toward the windows. "Have none of you looked outside?"

Frances quickly turned toward the nearest window

and was shocked to see a number of people in buggies or wagons, driving in the same direction as the train on a road parallel to the tracks. They were not dressed as elegantly as the people in New York. There were no top hats or canes to be seen among the men, and the women— many of whom wore broad-brimmed hats to shield their faces from the sun—were wrapped in shawls rather than elegant woolen coats. As Frances and the other children on the train stared at them, the people smiled and waved eagerly.

"Are they coming to see us?" Peg's voice was a squeak.

"Yes, and many more with them," Andrew said.

"All those people! How did they know we were coming?" a boy asked.

"Letting them know about you was part of my job," Andrew explained. "I put an advertisement in the *St. Joseph Weekly West* that told about the society's placing-out program. We received a response immediately, so I set up a committee of three prominent St. Joseph citizens to approve applicants. The next step was to bring you to St. Joe."

"Will we all live in St. Joseph?" someone asked.

"No. Most of you will live on nearby farms. A few of you will probably be adopted by families who live across the Missouri River in the Kansas Territory. And because we're so close to the borders of Iowa and Nebraska Territory, some of you might even find homes with families there."

Frances could feel the shudder that ran through Megan's body as she squeezed close and held tightly to Frances's hand. She heard Danny murmur again, "You and me together, Mike. Right?"

Curiosity and excitement overcame Frances's fear. She

pressed against the car window to see the busy, noisy town. Horseback riders, wagons, and foot traffic crowded the streets, just as they did in New York. But in St. Joseph, the streets were dirt, and few of the buildings were higher than two stories. The other children pushed to the windows, pointing and yelling as the train chugged into the station and rattled to a stop.

Many of the passengers on their car paused before leaving to say good-bye to the children and wish them well.

Captain Taylor came to where Frances stood with Mike and solemnly shook hands with both of them. He turned toward Mike. "Remember that the West is a place for new beginnings. You may think that you sacrificed your reputation, but you did not. It's what you make of your future that will count. And I believe that you'll have a good future, because you're a fine young man."

Mike blinked in surprise. "No one's called me a fine young man since my father died."

"Then it's time they did," Captain Taylor said. He placed a firm hand on Mike's shoulder. "I hope I will see you again. If either of you boys ever wants to get in touch with me, remember that I'll be at Fort Leavenworth, which is on the Kansas side of the Missouri River, about a day's ride south of St. Joseph."

"Thank you, sir," Mike said, and Frances nodded.

She and Mike stood silently for a moment, watching the captain leave the car. The station was a confusion of passengers, porters, and freight. Frances wished she could shrink back and disappear. She wondered if Mike were as frightened as she was.

"All right, children," Andrew called as soon as the adult passengers had left the railcar. "Let's get up here and form a line. We'll walk together over to one of the churches where people will come to meet you."

Holding tightly to Petey's hand as he managed the steep steps from the railroad car, Frances paused to look around the station. People were crowded on the platform in front of the small wooden building that served as a depot. Many of them were smiling. A few waved at the children. But here and there she saw someone appraising them the way Ma sometimes studied the greengrocer's cabbages. Which was the roundest, the heaviest? Which was the best?

Katherine turned to the children. "There's Jeff Thompson." She quickly corrected herself. "Mr. Merriweather Jeff Thompson, that is. He's the mayor of St. Joseph, elected just last year."

The mayor beamed at the children and began a speech of welcome. Frances was so distracted she only heard bits and pieces of the speech. ". . . the fine work of the Children's Aid Society . . . the good, upstanding people who are making a sacrifice to—"

Sacrifice? Frances thought. *That's the word Ma had used.* Her mother's sacrifice had been to give her children away, while these people's sacrifice was to keep them. Frances didn't understand it.

The mayor had just finished thanking Andrew and Katherine for their part in the undertaking when he was interrupted by the shouts of a short, thin boy dressed in a leather jacket and breeches. A wide-brimmed felt hat was pulled down on his head, the front of the brim fastened so that it stood straight up. Frances guessed that he was no older than fifteen or sixteen. He shoved his way through the crowd, holding aloft empty leather saddlebags and shouting importantly, "Make way!"

Mr. Thompson looked surprised for just an instant.

90

Then he said to the crowd, "Make a path for Billy Cody. The pony express must go through."

"Pony express! The mail to California!" Mike whistled through his teeth and pointed to a poster that was nailed on a nearby post:

WANTED: Young Skinny Wiry Fellows, not over eighteen. Must be expert riders willing to risk death daily. Orphans preferred. Wages $25 per week. Apply Central Overland Express.

"I could learn to ride," Mike said.

A man standing close by smiled and said, "It would take a while of practice and a great deal of skill to ride like Bill Cody and the other pony express riders."

Bill Cody ran from the depot, his saddlebags bulging with mail, and Frances could see him toss them over a stocky, saddled pony that was tied to a hitching rail. He leapt across the pony's back and galloped out of sight.

Andrew and Katherine shepherded the children into line and began their march to the church. Most of the adults in the crowd joined the walk, falling into line behind the children. A few curious town boys darted in to stare, sometimes pointing and snickering.

"We could take them on," Danny muttered to Mike, but Frances, with a warning scowl, pulled him back into line.

"They're of no account," she said, as though her feelings hadn't been hurt by the taunts. "We've got more important things to tend to."

The wooden sidewalks clattered under their feet, and as they crossed the streets, the women—most of whom, Frances noted, were dressed in dark homespun—held up their skirts to keep them out of the dust, stepping carefully over deep wagon ruts and horse droppings. Breaking the mingled odors of sweat and leather and dust were the gusts of a breeze that carried the damp, pungent fragrance of river water and wet grasses.

There was so much to see that Frances kept looking from side to side, occasionally stumbling: Indians, wrapped in blankets; men called frontiersmen, as brown as their deerskin jackets and leggings; people on horseback; even a team of oxen pulling a huge, canvas-covered wagon, pans and tools dangling from each side. At the western end of the street, Frances could see the glimmering water of the Missouri River, crowded with boats of all sizes.

The parade of children turned another corner and came to a large wooden building, which was painted white and topped by a steeple and cross. Andrew opened wide the double doors, and Katherine led the children to a raised platform at the far end of the room. A piano and stool were at one end, a carved, dark-stained pulpit at the other, and a deep red curtain hung over the back wall. Two rows of wooden chairs had been placed across the platform to face the room.

"Please find a seat on one of the chairs," Katherine directed.

Frances, terrified that Petey and she would be separated, held him on her lap and wrapped her arms protectively around him.

To Frances's right sat Peg, then Danny, who inched his chair closer to Mike's. Mike sat stiffly, his face so pale with fear that his freckles stood out like blots of splattered ink. Frances wished she could comfort him— Megan, too, who was on her left, her knuckles bone-white as she gripped the edge of the wooden seat—but

Frances was so frightened she was unable to think of what to do.

Little Clara, her hair bow now hanging crookedly over one eye, had climbed onto the chair next to Megan's. She stared with awe at the audience. "Look at all them eyes!" she whispered.

Frances felt herself drawn to look at the people in the room, fearfully searching one face, then another, for hopeful signs. Round or long, wrinkled or plumply red-cheeked, bushy-eyebrowed or scruffily bearded, no matter; every pair of eyes in every face stared intently at the children. Frances couldn't tell what they were thinking. She tried to look away, but couldn't. For a moment she felt dizzy, and her stomach churned. Desperately, she held Petey even more tightly. Who were all these strangers? Would any of them choose the Kelly children to be their own? What if no one wanted them? What would happen to them then?

9

THE ROOM WAS filled with spectators when Andrew stepped to the front of the platform and introduced himself. "I know most of you have heard about the work of the Children's Aid Society and the placing-out program that was organized six years ago by Charles Loring Brace," he said. "And I know that you're eager to meet the children, so I'll begin the introductions right away." He turned and offered a reassuring smile to the children. "I'm going to ask each of you to stand as I call out your name and your age," he said. "We want these folks to know who you are."

He began with the children in the front row. Just as Frances was deciding whether it was better to go through the introduction first and get it over with or to have time to prepare, Andrew reached the Kellys.

"Megan Eileen Kelly, twelve years old."

Megan almost didn't make it. Her legs wobbled just

before she plopped back on her chair. Frances reached out to touch her sister, but suddenly, "Francis Martin Kelly" boomed in her ears, and—with Petey still in her arms, squirming to clutch her tightly around the neck— she stumbled to her feet.

"Francis is thirteen," Andrew said, "and he's holding his little brother, Peter John Kelly, who is six years of age."

As hundreds of eyes examined her, Frances felt her face grow hot with embarrassment. Her stomach lurched. If she didn't sit down, fast, she was going to be sick. No! She wouldn't let herself. She took a deep breath and dropped to the chair, grateful that Andrew had called Peg's name.

Peg seemed more curious than frightened, studying the people in the audience as intently as they were studying her, and Danny jumped up with his chin out and head held high. It seemed nothing could keep Danny down, but Mike wasn't the jaunty, confident boy she knew so well. As Andrew announced, "Michael Patrick Kelly, almost twelve years old," Mike barely managed to slide from his chair. He hung back, his shoulders slumped, as the audience examined him.

Frances longed to jump up and hug him and reassure him that everything would be all right, but she knew no more than any of the others if it were true. *Oh, Ma!* she thought furiously. *Did you have any idea what would happen to us when you sent us here? When you betrayed us?*

When the introductions finally ended, Katherine stayed on the platform with the children, but Andrew jumped to the floor of the room. People came to talk to him, and Frances could see them point to one of the children or another. Husbands and wives were deep in discussion all around the room. Even Mr. Crandon had come, and Frances watched for a while as he moved from group to group, leaning close to whisper. She realized in horror that each couple to whom he spoke would immediately dart a glance toward Mike. Andrew and Katherine were too busy answering questions to notice Mr. Crandon. If he were telling people that Mike had been a copper stealer, it would be very hard for Mike to find a home.

Frances searched the faces in the crowd. There had to be a good man and woman here who would ignore what Mr. Crandon said and who would want Mike because they could see what a fine son he could be. Frances hoped so with all her heart.

Frances watched as a large, blond man with a small, frail-looking wife spoke to Andrew, the wife clasping Andrew's arm in her eagerness. Andrew nodded, smiled, and led them to the platform directly in front of Danny and Peg.

Immediately after introductions had been made, Mr. Alfrid Swenson asked Danny, "Do you think that small sister sitting next to you would be willing for the two of you to go with me and my wife?"

Mrs. Swenson's smile was so bright her gentle face glowed. "Please," she said, and held out a hand toward Peg.

White terror showed around the pupils of Danny's eyes, and his words rushed out in a stammer as he groped toward Mike. "Sir, my brother. Mike. If you could—could you take Mike, too? Please! You see we—we've never been parted so much as a day!"

Frances saw the sorrow in Mr. Swenson's face. "I'm sorry, son," he said. "We can only afford to take two children, and we wanted a boy and a girl."

"I won't eat much! Neither will Mike!" Danny pleaded.

Before Mr. Swenson, head down, turned completely away, Frances spoke up firmly. "Danny," she said, "we knew from the start what to expect. Mind your manners now, speak up smartly, and thank Mr. and Mrs. Swenson for offering to give you a good home. You, too, Peg."

"Frankie's right!" Mike spoke brusquely, almost angrily. "Get on with it, Danny."

Danny gulped and managed to whisper to Mr. Swenson, "Thank you, sir." Frances could see that Danny was making a valiant effort, and she was proud of him.

Peg solemnly reached for Danny's hand and climbed from her chair.

Andrew motioned to some chairs at the side of the room. "You can sit together and get acquainted," he said to the Swensons. As the children hesitated, he added, "Don't worry. You'll have time to say your good-byes to the rest of your family. You can exchange addresses before you go so that you can keep in touch with one another."

But Danny and Peg didn't move. They looked to Frances for help.

"Last night," Peg whispered, "I dreamed we all lived together in the same house."

"Dreams don't often come true." Frances heard herself echoing Megan's words. "Little one, I know this must be the best for you, or I wouldn't let you go. Do you understand?"

The corners of Peg's mouth turned down, but she nodded.

"Maybe someone will want Mike and me together." Danny carefully kept his voice low, so the Swensons couldn't hear, but Frances saw rebellious tears ready to spill from his eyes.

Frances wanted to sweep the two of them into her

arms and hold them tightly, but she knew they would have a good home with the Swensons, and she was glad they were together. She had to be as strong as Ma would have been.

"If they did, they would have spoken up by now," she said, her words masking the terrible ache in her heart. "You need a home, and it's my thinking that Mr. and Mrs. Swenson will give you a good one. They want to get to know you, so go with them now. Don't keep them waiting."

Mrs. Swenson's eyes were blurry with tears as she turned to Frances. "I'm so sorry," she said. "We would love to take all of your family, but—but—we're far from rich, and there are so many of you. If we only could . . . Please believe me."

"Don't be sorry, ma'am," Frances said. "We've known that we'd be separated. But we'll see one another again, and of that I'm sure. For now, each of us must go where we're wanted, and that's the all of it."

"Thank you," Mrs. Swenson whispered. She held out her arms to Peg, who stepped into them, allowing herself to be lifted from the stage. Peg and Danny walked to the side of the room with the Swensons.

Some of the other children already had left the stage. The older boys—those near the top limit of fourteen—had been chosen quickly, probably, Frances guessed, because they'd be a big help on a farm.

A pleasant-faced couple, squared and solid, glanced at Frances, and she eagerly sat up a little straighter, brushing Petey's blond curls back from his forehead and smoothing his collar. They seemed to be nice people, and they were discussing Petey and her. She held her breath. But their gaze moved on to Flora in the second row. They whispered together for a moment, then happily nodded agreement, and soon Frances saw Andrew lead them to where Flora sat waiting. Frances swallowed hard, but nothing would ease the painful tightness in her throat. *It's all right,* she told herself. *There's sure to be someone else.*

Katherine's voice sounded close to Frances's ear, and she turned quickly to see Katherine kneeling next to Megan, one arm around her shoulder. "Do you see that couple standing back there with Andrew and smiling at you?" she asked.

Megan nodded silently.

Frances searched them out. They were young. Even from the platform, Frances could see laugh crinkles at the corners of the woman's eyes. That was a good sign.

"Their names are Emma and Benjamin Browder, and they very much want you to come live with them, Megan. Mrs. Browder called you a beautiful little girl."

Megan smiled cautiously. "I've always been called plain. Maybe people are kinder in the West."

Katherine chuckled. "You're a lovely young lady. You just haven't noticed. In any case, the Browders arrived in town to get supplies, heard about the Orphan Train, and came to this meeting. As soon as they saw you they wanted you." Katherine paused. "I know them well. They'll love you, and you'll love them."

Frances leaned back in her chair, relieved. If Katherine spoke for them, then they must be good people.

"Do they live near here?" Megan asked, her eyes wide with hope.

"That's a problem," Katherine said. "They live many miles west of here in Kansas Territory. It would mean you'd be far from your brothers and sisters. You might see some of your family only once a year or so, when the Browders come to St. Joe for supplies and bring you with them. You do have a choice, Megan. You can go

99

with the Browders or wait to see if another couple asks for you."

Megan climbed stiffly from her chair, her face paler than before. She turned to Frances and whispered, "What can I hope for? I've always been a bad-luck penny."

"No, you're not!" Frances insisted.

But Megan had taken Katherine's hand. "I'll go with them," she told her.

The Browders were hurrying to the platform. Katherine introduced them to Megan.

Mrs. Browder laughed with delight. "There is so much I want to learn about you," she said to Megan. "Do you like books? Do you like to read?"

Megan blushed and glanced once more at Frances. "I'm not much at reading, ma'am," she replied hesitantly.

Frances ached for her sister. She knew how hard it would be for Megan to tell her new parents that she had always busied herself with chores, never learning to read.

But Mrs. Browder reached out and pulled Megan into her hug. "If you can't read, I'll teach you," she said. "You'll learn to love books as much as I do."

Megan's courage seemed to desert her. "Fr-Frankie!" she whimpered, turning toward her sister.

Frances couldn't speak. She knew she should give strength to Megan, but her throat was choked with tears, so she helplessly shook her head.

"There will be time for good-byes later," Katherine said. "Megan, let's find a spot for you and the Browders to talk to one another." She pointed. "Look, back there. I see some empty chairs."

Megan, her face tight with misery, walked hand in hand with Mrs. Browder to the back of the room. Frances was glad for Megan's sake. She could tell that the

Browders were kind people. Mrs. Browder looked at Megan as though she were a wonderful Christmas gift, so Megan would have a good home. In spite of herself, Frances felt her eyes fill with tears. How could she bear to part from her shy, loving sister, who had always been her dearest friend?

Many of the children had already left the platform when little Clara, her chin jutting out in determination, climbed down from her chair and marched to the front of the platform. To Frances's surprise, Clara faced the audience and shouted at the top of her lungs, "Doesn't anyone want to adopt *me*?"

A red-cheeked woman, as round as an apple, called, "I do! Oh, dear little *Liebchen*, I do!" and raced toward the platform, clutching her shawl around her with one hand and tugging her surprised husband behind her with the other. She enfolded Clara with such enthusiasm that all that Frances could see of Clara, as she was carried away, was her wobbly hair bow and her high-buttoned shoes.

Frances glanced to each side and felt her cheeks grow warm again. She, Petey, and Mike were the only ones left in the front row, and very few children were still seated in the second row. What would happen if they weren't chosen? Would they have to go back? Back to whom? The mother who didn't want them? The sudden, sharp memory of the judge telling Mike he'd have to go to Tombs Prison if he ever returned to New York City made her gasp aloud. Someone *had* to take Mike!

There was a slight commotion near the double doors as a rotund family—mother, father, and son—pushed their way into the room. The son was scowling as they entered; and the man's expression, as he looked up at the platform, became a matching scowl.

"I told you to hurry or we'd be late," he loudly complained to his wife. "Look! All the older, stronger boys have been chosen."

Frances shivered, wishing that these awful people would turn and leave. She didn't like them.

Andrew suddenly spoke to Frances. She swung to see a tall, pleasant-faced couple standing beside him. "Frankie," he said, "I'd like you to meet Jake and Margaret Cummings. They'd like you to come and live with them."

Frances's arms tightened around Petey, and she gulped back disappointment and frustration. Here, at last, were people who wanted her, and she had to turn them down. Her throat was suddenly so dry and tight that it hurt to speak. "Thank you," she whispered to the Cummingses. "But I can't accept your kindness. I must stay with my little brother."

Mrs. Cummings smiled and took a step forward. "We didn't make it clear. We want both of you. Little Peter, too."

Petey squirmed, trying to break Frances's strong grip. "My name is Petey," he said.

"We live close to the Missouri border in Kansas Territory, not far from St. Joe," Mr. Cummings said. He added to Petey, "We have a farm with cows and horses."

Petey pushed himself upright, nearly falling off Frances's lap. "Horses to ride?" he asked.

"That's right."

With a frantic wiggle Petey managed to jump from Frances's lap. He took Mr. Cummings's hand. "I would like to ride a horse," he said.

"Then so you shall," Mr. Cummings answered.

Mrs. Cummings smiled at Frances. "I'm afraid that my husband wants the two of you to come with us so much that he's not above using a bit of bribery. Please, Frankie, will you come home with us?"

"Yes," Frances said quietly. *Mike?* she thought. *What will I do about Mike?* But she had Petey to think of, too. "Thank you," she remembered to tell the Cummingses.

"Then suppose you find a spot to talk together," Andrew began.

He was interrupted by the family who had arrived late. The man slapped a pudgy hand on Andrew's shoulder, forcibly turning him. "That boy," he said, pointing at Mike. "We want to take him."

Frances, who had jumped from the platform, whirled to look at Mike. He was the only child left of those who had come on the Orphan Train. His face was red with embarrassment, and Frances knew he was holding back tears with great difficulty. Her heart breaking, Frances took a step toward Mike, but the fat woman pushed between them.

Frances saw a frown draw Andrew's eyebrows together. "Mr. and Mrs. Friedrich," he said, "you understand that these children are to be treated like family members. They are not to be used as hired hands."

"Of course, of course," Mrs. Friedrich said. "He'll be another son to us. We'll give the boy good food." She smiled and glanced quickly at her husband. "The boy needs only some good food to make him grow tall and strong."

"Our own son works beside me on our farm. I will not ask more of the boy than of my son. But it makes no matter. We have been approved by the committee," Mr. Friedrich stated, as though that should settle it. He asked Mike, "What is your name, boy?"

"Michael Kelly, sir," Mike said.

Mr. Friedrich turned to Andrew. "Where are the pa-

---

pers we are to sign? It is almost a two-hour ride back to our farm. We don't want to waste any time."

But Andrew looked carefully at Mike. "Do you want to go with them, Mike?" he asked. "It's your choice."

Frances listened for his answer as intently as Andrew did.

Mike looked about him at the otherwise empty platform, and Frances could see that he tried to put on a brave face. "It seems to be my only choice, Mr. MacNair," he said. "Yes, I'm game for it."

"Frankie? Are you coming?" Mrs. Cummings put a hand on Frances's shoulder, urging her toward where Mr. Cummings and Petey were waiting.

"Yes, ma'am. Just one minute, please," she said. She squeezed past Mrs. Friedrich to reach Mike and hugged him. "Go with them only if you really want to," she whispered.

"It couldn't be as bad as if I'm sent back," he mumbled against her ear.

"They don't seem like very kind people."

"Have you ever known me not to be able to hold my own?" He pulled away, squared his shoulders, and attempted a smile.

"You can say good-bye later," Andrew reminded them, so Frances reluctantly let go of her brother's hand and followed Mr. Cummings.

All of us have homes, just as Ma wanted, Frances thought, but she gave a glance back at Mike, hoping his new family would turn out to be better people than she guessed them to be.

The next few minutes were a blur of new faces, voices, and papers to sign. Then Katherine and Andrew came to stand in front of Frances.

"Katherine and I will stop by the Cummingses' farm

in a few days," Andrew told her. "Some small tools Jake ordered haven't come in. They're due on the next steamboat from St. Louis."

Katherine interrupted. "We'll deliver them ourselves. It will be a good excuse for a visit."

"I'll be so glad to see you!" Frances blurted out to Andrew before she thought. She tried hard not to blush at her eagerness.

"And so will we," Margaret Cummings said and explained to Frances, "We're all very good friends."

Katherine gave Frances a folded sheet of paper. "I wrote down your brothers' and sisters' addresses, and I've given them yours. You can keep in touch with them by letter until the next time you meet." She held out a hand to Frances. "Mr. Friedrich is eager to get back to his farm, so now would be a good time for you children to say good-bye to one another."

Peg dashed toward her, and Frances dropped to her knees to throw her arms around her littlest sister.

"I want you to come, too!" Peg cried.

"I can't, love," Frances whispered against her hair. "But you'll have Danny. The two of you will be together."

Danny squeezed them both so tightly it was painful. "I know how much you're hurting inside," Frances told him, "and I'm proud of you, Danny." Danny's body shook in a long, deep shudder, and she could tell he was fighting back tears.

Megan ran to them, wrapping her arms around Frances's neck. "I'll miss you so terribly much!" she cried as she clung to Frances. "I'll be all alone!"

"No, no, you won't," Frances murmured. "You'll have the fine people you'll be going with. They'll take good care of you. You won't be alone."

"But I won't be with you!"

105

"Oh, Megan!" Frances cried. She shut her eyes against the burning pain of tears she refused to shed. "Write to me," she said, "and I'll write to you."

"I can't write!" Megan wailed.

Frances quickly soothed her. "But you'll learn. Now you'll have a reason to learn. Your—your new mother will help you, and until you do she'll read my letters to you and—"

Megan burst out, "I don't want a new mother! Oh, Frances, can't we go home?"

Her words were a slap that shook sensibility back into Frances. She straightened. "No," she said. "Face the truth, Megan. We can't."

Megan stopped crying and blinked at Frances, who sounded so bitter she startled herself. "Megan," Frances said more softly, "Megan, you know that I meant—"

But Mike rushed to hug them, and Frances could feel the sobs that shook his body. Peg began to whimper, and Petey wailed.

Danny clung to Mike and cried, "What will I do without you, Mike?"

Mike just shook his head, snuffling and trying to smile at Danny. "You'll do just fine, my lad," he said. "Better than ever without me."

Danny shook his head as though he didn't believe those words any more than Mike did. "What about you, Mike?" he asked. "How will things work out with you?" He glanced suspiciously at the Friedrichs, and Frances knew that she wasn't the only one who was concerned about what kind of home they'd make for Mike.

"Have you ever known me to be down-and-out?" Mike retorted. He gave Danny a playful shove.

But Danny didn't return it. "Mike," he murmured as

tears rushed to his eyes, "I'll never be the same without you nearby."

With a cry Mike dove into Danny, burying his head in Danny's shoulder, and Frances reached over to enfold her brothers.

Suddenly Frances felt a hand on her shoulder, and Andrew said, "It's time to go now."

Megan and Peg only squeezed in more tightly, but Frances struggled to break free and get to her feet. She wiped her eyes on the back of one hand and gave a loud sniffle.

"Mr. MacNair is right," she said firmly. "We've had our chance to say good-bye, and now we mustn't keep our new families waiting any longer."

"Frankie?" Megan whispered.

"Good-bye, sister." Frances gave her one last kiss and a tentative smile. "I don't know when we'll be together again, but I'll write to you. Often!"

Megan, subdued, allowed herself to go with the Browders. Mrs. Browder's own eyes were as red as Megan's as she took Megan's hand.

The Swensons gathered up Danny and Peg, and with a last tearfully murmured "I'm sorry," from Mrs. Swenson to Frances, they hurried from the room.

"Be quick with you, Michael!" Mr. Friedrich said. "You should be a man and not waste time with foolish tears."

Mike shivered, and Frances reached out to rest her hands on his shoulders. She looked toward the Friedrichs. "If ever you need me, Michael Patrick, I'll come," she said firmly. "I won't be far away."

Michael stood as tall as he could and tried to smile. "I'll make do," he told her. "Nothing's going to get the best of me. I'm starting a new life in the West with a new family." He paused and for just an instant regained his cocky grin, adding, "And shouldn't you now be saying, Frankie Kelly, 'and that's the all of it?'"

"Be off with you, Mike," she said, answering his smile and trying hard to keep the tears from returning.

She felt a strong hand take her own, and she looked up to meet Jake Cummings's warm eyes. Petey, held high in his arms, looked to Frances for reassurance. "Ready?" Jake asked. "We've got a long ride ahead of us."

"I'm ready," Frances said with determination. But she trembled, because the words were nothing more than a brave lie.

10

"FRANKIE! FRANKIE, WAKE up! We're almost home!"

Frances struggled to a sitting position as Margaret's voice penetrated her dreams. She rubbed her eyes, then reached for Petey, who laughed.

"I'm up here on the big seat!" he crowed. "You slept for a long, long, *long* time!"

Frances knelt to look ahead and saw the road curve, leading upward past what looked like a forest.

Jake half turned to glance at her, then looked back at the road. "Cottonwoods near the water," he said, "but that's a good oak-hickory stand ahead. Lucky for us, the drought hasn't hit the east part of Kansas too hard."

"Drought?" Frances asked.

"It's been a dry year for folks who've settled farther west. To keep a farm going, you need plenty of rain. Not too much, not too little, just enough to soak the ground at the right times and help the crops grow to their peak."

Margaret laughed. "You sound like a real farmer."

"I thought he was a farmer," Frances said in surprise.

"Mr. Cummings has two horses," Petey offered helpfully, "so he must be a farmer."

"That's right, Petey," Jake said. "I am, but I wasn't until just six years ago. I taught at a university, Margaret was a teacher in a primary school, and we lived in New England—in the Commonwealth of Massachusetts, to be exact. Then a group of us decided to come to Kansas to homestead."

Frances was still puzzled. She grabbed for the side of the wagon to steady herself as the wagon dipped into a rut in the dirt road. "Did you get tired of the work you were doing?" she asked.

"No," Margaret said. "Someday I'd love to teach again, but we were needed in Kansas."

"Do you know what slavery is, Frankie?" Jake asked.

Frances pictured the black man being led away in chains at the train station. "Yes," she answered.

"Our country's national lawmakers worked out what they called a compromise—the Missouri Compromise. It gave us an equal number of states who accepted slavery and states who didn't. With a new Free State and new territories added since then, the balance has shifted. The people who live in those territories want them to be free-soil, but the Southerners say no. The only way to succeed in making Kansas a Free State is to become a homesteader and have a voice in Kansas policy."

"We came to Kansas because we believe that slavery is wrong," Margaret said. "Many people have sacrificed the comfortable lives they had in the East for this cause."

Sacrifice! That word again. Frances nodded as Margaret spoke, but it was hard to understand. Frances was sure she would rather be a teacher than a farmer. To work with books, to learn from them, and to help others learn—that would be a wonderful job. She wondered if they missed the jobs they had and the land they came from. No. She couldn't understand.

"We'll soon be home," Margaret said, "and I know you're going to enjoy your welcome."

"Welcome?" Frances asked.

"Some of our neighbors planned to come to meet our child—our children—you. We'll have quite a party."

"What's a party?" Petey asked.

"You know," Frances said, "like when Ma and Da would sing Irish songs, and we'd drink hot tea with milk and sugar."

Margaret smiled. "At this party our friends from all the nearby farms will come, each of them bringing home-cooked dishes, and roasted meat, and fruit pies. There'll be other children to play with, and games, and good conversation."

"We've never been to that kind of a party," Frances said.

"Oh!" For a moment Margaret looked distressed. Then she gave Petey a little hug and said, "Then this will be your first Kansas party. I can promise that you'll enjoy it!"

The river was a thin ribbon of mirrored sunlight below and to the east as the horses turned off the dirt road into a narrower lane and slowly tugged the wagon up a slight rise. Ahead, beyond a half dozen wagons lined up near the lane, Frances could see a two-story wood house, bright with white paint. Just to the right of it was a small log cabin, and to the left of it was a barn, larger than the house. She sat erect to study the buildings. The house was like a palace compared to the building in which she had lived in New York. It was every bit as grand as the house she had built in her dreams.

Margaret's voice rose in a happy lilt as she explained, "Our house is new. A real house again! We've had five good years and one fair one of corn and wheat, and we were able to build." With pride she added, "And we have our own well! We no longer have to carry water from the river."

Two boys dashed around the side of the house, stopping when they saw the wagon. Both were blond; one was tall and one stocky. They were dressed much as Frances was, in collarless shirts, loose jackets, and trousers. The tall one stayed to wave while the other ran inside the house, calling out and banging the door behind him. As they pulled to a stop near the barn, the door to the house opened, and a flurry of children and adults ran outside. With them ran a large, shaggy-haired brown dog.

"A dog!" Petey shouted. "Is it yours?"

"Yours, too," Jake said. "His name is Barker."

Jake held Frances's hand as she jumped from the wagon. Margaret was being hugged, and everyone was talking at once, exclaiming over Frances and Petey.

"Two! Aren't you lucky!"

"What wonderful boys!"

"What are their names? Tell us about them."

Petey, suddenly shy, dove for Frances and wrapped his arms around her neck. She was glad to hold him. It gave her a chance to duck her head against his so that she wasn't facing everyone at once. She could peek through the corners of her eyes to examine them, especially the boys who seemed to be about her age and who were frankly examining her.

"What's the matter with you? Can't you say any-thing?" the stocky boy asked Frances.

"There's nothing to say," Frances answered back.

"Huh! You come from Boston," the boy said.

"Naw, Elton," the other said. "All those orphans were coming from New York."

"He talks like some of them who come from Boston."

"He talks Irish. That's what you hear. It's Irish."

"And proud of it!" Frances said, raising her head and attempting to stare them down.

One of the women, who had tied a billowing white apron over her long homespun skirt, gave a little tap on the stocky boy's shoulder, saying, "Elton, Johnny, mind your manners. These boys will be your neighbors and friends. Make them feel at home."

Margaret put an arm around Frances and Petey. "I know you'd like to get acquainted and play with the other children for a while, so I'll show you your new home later."

"I could see it now," Frances said quickly, anxious to escape these strange faces.

"No. Just have a good time for yourselves," Margaret said as though she thought Frances were only trying to please. "We'll have dinner on the table in a short time. I know you must be very hungry."

Already the women had set up a large table covered in white cloths. Margaret bustled off to join them. Some of the men went with Jake to store the wagon and help with the horses.

"Want to play tag?" a small girl asked Petey. Without a word to Frances, Petey wiggled out of her arms and raced off with the younger children, all of them shriek-ing at the top of their lungs. Barker, living up to his name, ran with them.

113

Johnny and Elton ran off, too, shoving, poking, and yelling at each other, ignoring Frances. For this she was thankful. But some of the women began darting little concerned glances at her, so she went after the boys, wanting only to get away from all these people.

As she rounded the corner of the house she discovered she was alone. Enjoying the silence, she gladly leaned against a nearby elm tree. The Cummingses' land was beautiful. The house overlooked a large meadow dotted with trees, a few of them still green, many bright with orange and yellow leaves. To one side lay a field of black soil rising in rows of low mounds separated by shallow valleys, cleared except for a scattering of dried stalks. Next to the back of the house was a garden, and she could see rounds of orange and yellow poking through green vines. Were they squash? Pumpkins? She had eaten squash and pumpkin both but had never imagined what they looked like before they arrived in huge piles at the greengrocer's shop. If only she could show this to Megan or Ma. She pushed the thought that would lead to tears from her mind.

A bright spot of color lying on a patch of grass near her feet caught her eye, and she bent to pick it up. It was a doll, made all of cloth. Frances had never seen anything like it. It was so different from the elegant dolls with china faces and silk dresses in the store windows of New York. This homely doll, with its embroidered eyes and smile and hair of tangled brown yarn, went straight to Frances's heart. For just an instant, she held the doll close.

"Whatcha doing with a girl's doll?" The mocking voice came from just behind her.

Frances whirled to face Elton and Johnny. "Never

saw one of these before," Frances mumbled and dropped the doll to the ground.

Elton grinned. "You dropped your dolly. You ought to pick it up before it gets all dirty." He grabbed Frances's shoulder and pushed down hard.

But Frances was no stranger to bullies. Having learned well from Mike how to protect herself, she reacted instinctively. Twisting into Elton, she butted him in the stomach. She hooked a foot behind his and jerked. Elton landed on his back in the dirt.

"What's going on, boys?" A woman who had come from around the corner of the house wiped her hands on her apron and stared at them suspiciously. "You're not fighting, are you?"

"No, ma'am," Frances said. "Just having fun."

The woman looked a little dubious but said, "Dinner's about ready. You can wash up by the back door."

As the woman walked away, Frances reached down, grabbed Elton's elbow, and pulled him to his feet. Dusting him off much harder than necessary, she murmured, "Want to talk any more about dollies? Or have you got enough sense to talk about something else?"

"Whatcha get so mad for?" the boy answered. "I was just making some fun."

Johnny folded his arms and appraised Frances. "Did you learn to fight like that in New York City?"

"That's where I'm from," Frances said.

"How'd you do that thing with your feet?" Johnny asked. "That was fast. Could you show me how to do it?"

"Children! Everyone! Come to dinner!" one of the women called.

"C'mon! Let's eat!" Elton shoved Johnny so hard he

nearly knocked him off his feet. He was off in a moment, Johnny right behind him.

Frances relaxed, once more leaning against the tree and letting out a long, slow breath. That was close. In the future she'd have to be a lot more careful.

Frances splashed her face and neck with cold water from the basin, then dried herself with the towel that hung on a hook over the wooden bench. The water felt good, and she realized how hungry she had become.

She walked around the house to join the others. Petey was sitting on the grass with some other children, a filled tin plate between his legs.

A short, plump woman with smiling eyes greeted Frances, propelled her toward the table, and handed her a plate. Frances struggled to remember the woman's name. Mrs. Mueller. Johnny's mother. Yes, that was it.

"Help yourself, Frankie!" Mrs. Mueller said.

What a feast! At first Frances could only stare at the baskets and plates that covered the table. She had never seen so much food in one place. At the far end of the table were large bowls of red apples and stacked loaves of brown bread, with pots of honey and butter near them. Nearby were bowls and pans piled with meats and vegetables she didn't recognize, but that were so fragrant the smell of them caused her stomach to rumble.

Mrs. Mueller patted Frances's shoulder and said, "Maybe some of our food is strange to you. But I think you'll like it. Over there in the brown dish is game-bird pie." She named one dish after another: cured and roasted pork hocks, pickled carrots, Indian cornmeal pudding— from which rose the tantalizing fragrance of molasses— and cold sliced potatoes seasoned with a sauce of bacon drippings and onions. "And squash pie, especially for

Margaret," she finished proudly. "That's a real favorite with New Englanders."

"Aren't you from New England, too?" Frances asked.

Mrs. Mueller shook her head. "No. My husband and I settled our land even before these good friends arrived. We live just over the border in Nebraska Territory." The laugh lines around her eyes crinkled as she giggled and whispered, "But I didn't forget my own favorite—the potatoes. It's my mother's recipe."

Frances continued to stare at the food. Would her brothers and sisters be eating this well? She was greedy to taste the fine dishes but guiltily remembered the watery cabbage and mealy potatoes that Ma had to eat. But Mrs. Mueller heaped a plate for Frances and pushed it into her hands. "Eat well," she said. "You need a few good meals to build those young muscles."

Some of the children had carried their plates and forks to the front porch, where they sat in a row, dangling their legs over the edge, intent on the good food they were eating. The men had taken their plates inside the house, and Frances could hear the low, comforting rumble of their deep voices. The women didn't sit still for long anywhere but bustled back and forth between the kitchen and the table, sometimes stopping to fill their plates and stand, eating and chatting, for a few moments.

Frances didn't know where to take her plate. The boys were too rough, and she couldn't sit with the girls. They wouldn't want her anyway. Thankful that no one was watching her, she slipped into the parlor, where the men were seated, and sat on the floor near the side of the fireplace. It was a warm, inviting room, and Frances had a strange sense of belonging there. As she looked around she understood why. The embroidered pillows on the chairs and the lace curtains at the windows came from the house she had built in her dreams. It was perfect, except for one thing: her family was not there with her.

The men began to speak of Abraham Lincoln. "He's not much to look at, being a long bean pole of a man, but he's a mighty fine orator," Mr. Mueller said.

"You heard him speak?" a younger man asked.

"Yes, and met him, too. Last year he came to St. Joseph on the side-wheeler boat *Emile*, on his way to Council Bluffs."

"You know what it means if Lincoln is elected," someone said, and the conversation turned to the possibility of war among the states and to terrible, bloody raids made over the past few years along the Kansas-Missouri border by both proslavery Missourians and Kansas abolitionist jayhawkers.

"Lincoln will do away with slavery," Jake said, and the others agreed.

The conversation was interesting, but the plate of food, with its mingled spicy, sweet, and pungent fragrances, demanded Frances's attention. She decided to try a bite of pie first and didn't stop until she had devoured every crumb. Then she attacked the rest of the meal, forgetting her manners and stuffing herself full of pork and potatoes and some strange—but delicious—things she still couldn't name. It was only when the plate was as clean as though she had licked it, and her stomach round and tight against her trousers, that Frances leaned back against the wall and really paid attention to what the men were saying.

Someone was talking about the "Underground Railroad." She imagined a train with tracks that rattled and rocked along through caves and caverns.

"Until the Fugitive Slave Act is abolished, the Underground Railroad is the only answer," Mr. Mueller said.

There was silence for a moment, then a man with gray in his hair spoke up. "Don't forget, Klaus, that taking part in helping a slave escape is against the law. There are severe penalties."

"How can you balance penalties against helping a man to gain his freedom?"

"You would risk going to prison?"

A young man leaned forward and spoke earnestly, holding up a hand to interrupt Mr. Mueller. "Wait. Think for a moment before another word is said. We are all neighbors and good friends here. We can trust one another. But we still should not be too outspoken. We are all working within the law to help Kansas become a Free State. That is the first step."

"The process is slow," Mr. Mueller grumbled.

The man's tone became more deliberate. "None of us knows anyone who is a part of the Underground Railroad. Let us keep it that way."

Jake stood up. "More coffee, Klaus? William? Henry? Let me fill your cups."

The young man bounced to his feet. "Real coffee, and not roasted rye! This is quite a party!"

"Aha!" Mr. Mueller said, his mood changing to match the others'. "Wait until the Christmas season. *That* will be a party. Frieda will bake a Christmas cake big enough to feed the whole countryside!"

"With plenty of raisins?" someone asked, laughing.

"Yes, raisins! And, Henry, we'll expect you to bring your fiddle."

"I would bring it, even if you hadn't asked me to!"

A few minutes later the young man put down his cup

and said, "It's time for me to collect my family and prepare to head for home."

"Also for me," another one said.

By this time all the men were on their feet. Some of the women began hurrying into the house, and Frances made her way to the kitchen. She could never have imagined a kitchen like this one.

It was a large, square room with a huge fireplace at the far end. A row of long-handled iron skillets, two large kettles, ladles, a toasting fork, and some other cooking tools hung on pegs above the fireplace. Next to the hearth stood a cupboard with double doors. An ornate, round wood stove was at one side of the kitchen, a cloth-covered table and some ladder-back chairs at the other. Near the center of the room was a sturdy worktable, and against the inside wall were shelves laden with stoneware jars and crocks of all sizes, tinware, and kitchen tools that Frances had never seen before. The room was cozy with the odors of food, the leftovers of which were now being parceled out among the women and tucked into cloth-covered baskets. *Oh, Ma!* Frances thought. *You wouldn't believe this wondrous kitchen unless you could see it with your own two eyes!*

It hurt too much to think of Ma. Frances knew she had to get busy to force her mind to go in another direction. With a folded towel to protect her hands, she swung out the iron crane from inside the fireplace and removed a steaming kettle from its pot hook, pouring the water into two large, metal bowls that had been set on one of the tables. The youngest woman—Mrs. Busby—thanked Frances. Into one of the bowls Mrs. Busby stirred a dollop of soap from a jar of scrapings and water that sat on the windowsill. She then added a small amount of cold water to both bowls.

Frances immediately dumped the tray of used forks and knives into the soapy water and began to rub them clean.

Mrs. Busby's eyes opened wide with surprise. "Where did you learn to wash dishes like that?" she asked.

Puzzled, Frances frowned. "Am I doing it wrong?"

"Oh, no," Mrs. Busby said. "It's just that you don't often find boys willing to do women's work."

Frances fumbled for the right words to cover her mistake. "If work needs to be done, what difference does it make who does it?" She ducked her head and scrubbed hard at the utensils.

"My, my," Mrs. Busby said. "I like the way you think, young man." She picked up a bleached flour sack and began to dry the utensils that had been washed and rinsed.

I've got to be more careful, Frances reminded herself, so when Margaret came to shoo Frances out to play with the other boys, she went without protest.

As she left the kitchen, Frances heard Mrs. Busby say to Margaret, "Frankie is a gentle boy," so she deliberately found Elton and picked a quarrel. They pummeled each other and rolled in the dirt, until two of the men pulled them apart.

"Just havin' fun," Elton mumbled to his father.

"Is that right, Frankie?" Jake asked.

Frances shook her head. "No, but the fight was my fault. I pushed him."

Mr. Mueller laughed loudly. "An honest answer. The boys are angry now, but in a few minutes they'll be friends."

Frances held out her right hand toward Elton. "Shake on it," she said.

Grudgingly Elton did. The sun had dipped low and

121

red in the western sky, and it was time for the party to end. Within a few minutes Elton and his family were in their wagon, heading for their own farm. The few families who had tarried shouted their good-byes, too, until the Muellers were the only guests who remained.

"They'll stay the night," Margaret explained to Frances, "because the ride back to their home would take them far too long. If you have no objections, we'll offer your bed to Klaus and Frieda. We'll put little Karl and Matthew in with Peter, and we'll lay pallets on the floor in front of the kitchen fireplace for you, Johnny, and Fred."

"A houseful of boys!" Mrs. Mueller laughed, waggling a finger at them. "And you must all go to sleep without chattering late into the night, because we have to rise early to begin our drive home."

As darkness fell, quilts and pillows were carried to the kitchen and piled on the floor near the fireplace. Barker curled up under the table by the wall as though to protect the spot that belonged to him.

Frances glanced around the kitchen. It was so different from home, where they lived in only one room and all the children shared one big bed. For just an instant Frances yearned with all her heart for her own home, with her brothers and sisters and Ma. Then she sharply reminded herself that this place was her home now, and she would do her best to accept the fact that there was no turning back.

Margaret paused to look at Frances. "Oh," she said. "I didn't think. You and Peter must want a bath after your long journey. Well, we can bring the tub into the kitchen and take care of that as soon as I have some water heated." She picked up the kettle and headed toward a large pottery crock of water.

Frances stumbled in front of Margaret, blocking her way. "No!" she cried. She tried to talk calmly. "Petey is much too tired," she said. She faked an open-mouthed yawn. "And so am I. Could we wait until tomorrow?"

Frances held her breath in suspense until Margaret shrugged and said, "If you'd rather."

"I'd *much* rather," Frances insisted.

Margaret glanced at Petey, who was almost asleep on his feet, too tired to protest being taken from Frances to be tucked into a strange bed. "I suppose you're right," Margaret said. She scooped Petey into her arms while Mrs. Mueller gathered Karl and Matthew and headed for the stairs.

Fred, who was a younger version of his brother Johnny, immediately pulled off his square-toed boots, his stockings, and his trousers and dove into one of the pallets. "Ha, ha!" he shouted. "I got the best spot!"

"That's what you think," Johnny said as he winked at Frances. "You got the quilt with the itchy, nasty old bedbugs in it."

Fred scrambled out of the quilts so fast he kicked the pallet apart. "Bedbugs? Where?" he demanded.

Johnny laughed loudly, and Fred angrily tried to make up the bed again, muttering, "You think you're so funny, but that was dumb. You're a dumb, stinkin' old skunk's bottom!"

Frances returned Johnny's grin. "I'm still hungry," Johnny said to Frances. "I'm going to get an apple. You want one, too?"

Frances took the apple that Johnny held out to her and followed him outside, sitting next to him on the stoop in the darkness.

"How old are you?" Johnny asked.

"Thirteen," Frances said.

123

Johnny sounded smug. "I'm fourteen."

"I'm near to fourteen."

"I'm near to fifteen." He paused, taking a large bite from the apple. "My pa and your new pa are best friends."

The apple cracked as Frances bit into it. Tart juice sprayed her face, and she wiped it away with the back of one hand.

"We used to live in Pennsylvania. That's near New York, where you come from," Johnny said. "But I don't remember it much, because I wasn't very old when we moved to Nebraska. Did you like traveling on a train?"

"Sort of and sort of not," Frances mumbled around a mouthful of apple. She swallowed hard and said, "At first it was different—all the new things to see. I never saw a farm before. But trains stop a lot to get water and wood, and they rock back and forth and rattle, and it's hard to sleep."

"That sounds boring."

"It was kind of boring, except for when we had to stop to put out a brushfire and when some outlaws robbed the train."

"Huh!" Johnny whirled to stare at Frances, his eyes gleaming in the darkness. "You're making that up!"

"Am not!"

"Then tell me. Tell me about the outlaws!"

"The fire first," Frances said. "I'll tell you about the outlaws later." *Much later*, she thought. She didn't want to tell him about Mike and what he had done. To make her story about the fire last longer, she put in everything she could remember, even the way the hot sparks shot from the smokestack on the train.

As she finished, Johnny let out a long whistle. "You're good at telling a tale! Tell about the outlaws now."

Frances shook her head. "I'll tell you some other

time. I'm ready to go to sleep." She stood up and walked around the stoop to the bench. Once more she washed her face and hands.

Johnny watched her. "How come you're washing up again? Nobody said you had to."

"We always washed up before going to bed. That was one of Ma's rules."

"Your ma? But—oh." Johnny quickly looked away, then turned and threw open the kitchen door.

Only the banked coals in the fireplace lit the kitchen. Frances took off her jacket, boots, and stockings and climbed under the quilts, as far away from Fred and Johnny as she could get. She pulled the quilt up to her chin. It was warm and cozy, and she burrowed deeply into it. She squeezed her eyes shut. Jake and Mr. Mueller still were talking in low tones in the parlor. Then the house was still, except for the creak-crack of the wooden stairs as the men went up to bed.

The house was filled with people, yet Frances had never felt so lonely. When would she see Megan again? And Peg and Danny and Mike? Although she tried to fight them back, hot tears spilled down her cheeks, and she gave a loud sniffle.

She heard Johnny turn toward her. "Ma said you had to leave your other brothers and sisters," he whispered. "If I had to leave Matt and Karl and even old froggy Fred over there, I'd cry, too."

Frances sniffled again and mumbled, "I don't mean to cry."

"My pa said it's all right to cry sometimes. He told me he cried once when he was a grown man and right out in front of everybody. He cried 'cause he saw a man get shot and killed."

Frances wiped at her eyes. "I'm sorry I woke you."

"You didn't wake me," Johnny said. "I couldn't sleep, thinking of the fine story you told about the fire." There was a long pause, then Johnny said, "Hey, Frankie. I'm glad we're friends."

"Me, too," Frances said, surprised that she really was glad.

The quilt at the far end rose in a quivering hump. "Close your big, ugly mouths," Fred growled. "I'm trying to sleep!"

Frances stuffed a fist in her mouth, suppressing a giggle, which turned itself into a yawn. The Cummingses were good people, and at least Petey was with her. She wouldn't let herself think of anything else. Frances yawned again and slid headfirst into sleep.

11

THE SKY WAS barely light when Frances, Johnny, and Fred were rousted out of bed.

For a moment Frances didn't know where she was. Her body was still caught in the rocking, jerking rhythm of the train. Instinctively she reached out for her family but was jolted awake as her fingertips met only the hard plank floor.

Megan, Mike, Danny, and Peg—were they all right? Had they awakened with eyes still burning from tears, as she had? And what was Ma doing? *Ma*, Frances thought. *Oh, Ma, what have you done to us? How could you have sent us so far away?*

"Get up, sleepyheads!" Mrs. Mueller called, and Frances forced herself to roll from under the warm quilt and pull on her stockings and boots.

Frances carried in armloads of wood for the stove and fireplace, while Johnny made a few trips to the well, filling the large pottery crock with water. Mrs. Mueller and Margaret bustled from table to stove, and before long everyone was eating hot buckwheat cakes with cane molasses and crisp pan sausage. Petey was so happy to be eating he didn't look at all sad or homesick.

Barker was the first to hear the hoofbeats. He rose to his feet and growled.

Margaret held up a hand for silence. "Riders," she announced.

Jake and Mr. Mueller pushed back their chairs and strode through the parlor to the front door.

"It's the marshal," Jake called. "A couple of men are with him."

Barker and the children raced after the men to the front porch, the women following. Frances saw Margaret and Mrs. Mueller glance at the men on horseback, then at each other with concern.

The marshal touched his hat to the women and smiled easily. "Mornin', Jake, Klaus. You got quite a passel of young'uns there."

"Meet our new sons," Jake said proudly. He picked up Petey and put an arm around Frances's shoulders before introducing them to Marshal Dawson.

The marshal was a big man, brown from the sun. He wore a broad-brimmed hat and a leather jacket that looked much like the ones Frances had seen on the frontiersmen in St. Joseph. The men who were with him were dressed the same way. Although the marshal had a friendly smile on his face, his two companions scowled. Both men carried rifles in slings on their saddles.

Margaret stepped forward. "Care for some breakfast, Marshal Dawson? Maybe a cup of coffee?"

"Well, maybe I—"

"We got business to take care of," one of the other men growled. "There's no time for that."

The marshal nodded reluctantly. "Jake, we're huntin' a pair of runaway slaves."

Mrs. Mueller sniffed contemptuously. "Bounty hunters!"

"Hush," Margaret whispered, but the men ignored her, and the marshal continued.

"We're pretty sure that they crossed the river somewhere below St. Joe and are probably headin' north into Canada. Big, strong fellow and a woman 'bout maybe five feet tall. Her mistress said the woman might a' been wearin' a shawl she give her. It's black with some blue flowers embroidered in one corner. You seen any sign of them, Jake?"

"No," Jake answered.

"All right, then." The marshal again reached up and touched the brim of his hat. "Mrs. Cummings, Mrs. Mueller."

"Just a minute!" snapped one of the men. "You're going to take his word for it?"

"No reason to doubt Jake's word," Marshal Dawson said.

"Well, I don't trust a one of these New Englander settlers." He twisted in his saddle to spit on the ground, wiped his mouth on his jacket sleeve, and stared hard at the group on the porch. His glance finally came to rest on Frances.

"How about you, boy?" he asked. "What do you know about these runaway slaves?"

"I don't know anything." Frances stared back at him, unblinking, until the man finally looked away.

The other bounty hunter leaned forward and made an effort to appear friendly. "Maybe you folks haven't heard there's a reward offered on the slaves."

No one answered.

He sat upright again and shrugged. "It's going to get worse around here for anybody who's helpin' slaves to escape." As though to prove his point, he pulled his rifle from its sling and held it ready, resting the stock against his right boot.

Marshal Dawson pulled on the reins, tugging his horse toward the left. "Sorry to have bothered you folks," he said. "You understand, the law's the law, and seeing that it's carried out is my job."

The men rode grudgingly with him. As soon as the marshal and the bounty hunters reached the road, Mr. Mueller glanced up at the sky. "We've overstayed our welcome. We'll help you with the chores."

"No need," Jake said. "You've got a long ride. Better get on your way."

Mr. Mueller gripped Jake's hand. "I know I'll be seeing you soon," he said.

The Muellers' horses were hitched to their wagon, and a covered basket of food was handed up.

The Cummingses waved good-bye until the Muellers' wagon had reached the road. Then Jake turned to Frances and Petey. "We're a little late in getting to the morning chores," he said. "Margaret and I have given thought to what you boys can do, and we worked out a list that shouldn't be too difficult to handle."

"I'll ride the horses," Petey offered.

"Not just yet." Jake smiled. "But Margaret will teach you to feed the chickens and gather the eggs, and you can help pull weeds in the vegetable garden."

Petey jumped up and down with excitement.

"But right now," Margaret said, "you can help me clean up the kitchen."

Frances quickly offered, "I can do that."

130

"I've got other chores for you," Jake told her. "The cows badly need milking, and then they must be taken out to pasture. You'll help care for the horses, feed the animals, and lend me a hand in the fields."

Frances grinned. Milk a cow? She would love to!

The two milk cows were bawling by the time Jake and Frances entered the barn. Jake pulled a stool next to the brown-and-white cow and placed a pail under her. "Over here, Frankie. Get close, where you can watch what I do."

Frances sidled up to the cow, who turned her head and stared. The cow was much larger than Frances had thought she'd be, and when she opened her mouth and bawled again, Frances jumped back.

"She won't hurt you," Jake said. He demonstrated to Frances what to do, and twin streams of milk shot into the pail. "It's easy," he said. "Hold your hands like this."

Frances took Jake's place on the stool and tried to copy Jake, squeezing hard.

But the cow stepped sideways in protest and knocked Frances off the stool. Frances's feet hit the pail, which toppled over. "Oh, no!" Frances cried.

Jake just laughed and helped Frances to her feet. He set the stool and pail back in place and said, "Try it again, and this time make your hands both firm and gentle."

Shaking, Frances sat on the stool. She kept a wary eye on the cow.

"Lean your head against her," Jake said. "It makes it easier for you, and old Clover likes it."

"That's her name?" Frances asked. "Clover?"

"That's it. Now give it a try."

Frances took a deep breath and stared back at the cow, who had turned to study her again. "Settle down,

Clover," she ordered. "Sure and this time I'll be doing it right." Frances pressed her cheek against the cow's warm body and began milking again. She tried to follow Jake's instructions and was delighted finally to hear the hiss and slap of milk into the pail. If only Da could have seen her. If only Ma could have tasted this warm, sweet milk. *Stop it!* Frances scolded herself. *Thoughts like that won't make it easier to get along here.*

"Good work," Jake said, and in a moment Frances heard him begin to milk the other cow. Soon there were two buckets of foamy milk to carry to the kitchen.

Frances worked hard, sweating in spite of the cool weather, as Jake taught her—with Barker's help—how to drive the cows into the meadow, chop wood, carry water, and clean the barn. He led her over a rise to a field rippling with yellow-green grasses.

"I'm experimenting with a patch of winter wheat," he said. "Not many have tried it yet, but those who have claim that it's more hardy than spring wheat."

"What's spring wheat?" Frances asked.

"It's wheat we'll plant in the spring along with oats and barley," Jake replied. "We'll harvest it in July. The winter wheat will be ready to cut in just a few weeks. One more job for you to learn to do."

"I can do it," Frances said.

Jake smiled. "It's easy to see that you're not afraid of hard work."

"I'm used to hard work," Frances said. She smiled as she realized those daily hours of scrubbing floors had built up muscles she was now very glad to have.

Margaret called to them from the house. Jake, resting a hand on Frances's shoulder, said, "Our midday meal will be ready, son."

Frances was no longer surprised to be called "son."

But she was surprised at how hungrily she wolfed down her food. It felt good to have a full stomach all the time. Ma had been telling the truth about that. But what was a full stomach compared with the emptiness left in her heart by the thought that she might never again see her family all together? She would never believe that Ma had done the right thing.

Frances Mary Kelly, stop it right now, she told herself. She had to keep busy, so busy that she didn't have time to think of such things. "What jobs do you have for me now?" she asked Jake.

Her eyes twinkling, Margaret put an arm around Frances's shoulders. "Jake can spare you for a little while," she said. "It's time for lessons."

"Lessons? You mean schooling?"

"That's right. We have no schoolhouse in the area yet, so I'll be your teacher, and we'll have daily lessons. I want my sons to be educated."

Real schooling! Frances could hardly believe her good luck. This was something that had always been so far beyond her reach that Frances had never dared to dream that she might someday go to school.

Margaret asked, "Can you read, Frankie?"

"Yes, ma'am," Frances said, proud that Da had taught her.

Margaret threw open one of the doors of the cupboard, where Frances could see at least a dozen books. She selected one, opened it, and brought it to Frances. "Let me hear you read this page."

Frances glanced at the cover of the book. *The School Reader, Third Book.* Then she looked at the page to which Margaret had opened the book and began easily to read aloud: "Lesson One, The Boy Rebuked by His Dog."

It was a funny story about a dog who willingly carried his mistress's basket when the lazy boy in the family did not hurry to obey his mother's command. Frances giggled as she reached the ending.

Frances put down the book and looked up at Margaret, who smiled with pleasure. Petey laughed at the story and shouted, "I'm going to teach Barker to carry a basket!" He dove under the table and tried to tug Barker into the room.

"Why, Frankie!" Margaret said. "You read very well! Then you have been to school."

"No, ma'am," Frances said. "Da taught me."

"He did a good job," Margaret said. "Did your parents teach you penmanship, spelling, and geography, too?"

"I can write some," Frances said. "But they didn't have time to teach us the rest."

Margaret beamed. "Then I'm going to have two pupils again." She pulled some paper from a drawer and put it on the table.

Frances touched the paper greedily. "Ma'am, could I use some of this to write to my brothers and sisters?"

"Of course!" Margaret said. "And to your mother, too."

Frances didn't answer. No one needed to know that she was still too angry to think of writing to her mother.

Jake turned at the door. "Once a week the postmaster in town sends the mail out. Your letters can be picked up then."

Later in the day the animals had to be cared for again. By the time supper was over Frances was tired, but she joined Jake in the parlor, sitting on a stool near his chair.

"Tell me about the Underground Railroad," she begged.

"It isn't underground, and it isn't a railroad," Jake

134

explained. "And it isn't something to be discussed with anyone else. It's a series of homes, known only by word of mouth to those involved, where escaping slaves are sheltered and cared for until it's safe to send them to the next home in the chain. When these people finally reach Canada, they have also reached freedom," Jake added.

"Do you work with the Underground Railroad? Is this house part of the chain?"

Jake paused a moment, then smiled. "There are things you don't need to know, son."

"I want to help, too," Frances said. "From the window of the train I saw a black man who had metal cuffs and chains around his wrists, and he was being led by two men who must have been bounty hunters. I'm sure he was a slave who'd been caught, and I felt so sorry for him. It wasn't fair!" Frances thought of the man who told her she couldn't read, the woman who spoke about her as if she weren't there. "We were never slaves, but I know how it is to be treated as if you had no feelings."

"We share the same opinions, Frankie," Jake said, and his pride in her shone in his eyes. "But helping escaping slaves is a dangerous job. It's not something in which a young boy should be involved."

Margaret came into the parlor, her sleeves rolled high on her arms. "I've just given Petey a bath, and now it's your turn, Frankie."

Frances gasped, and Margaret laughed. "I didn't mean that you'd need me to help you. If you need anything, just call on Jake."

"I won't need help!" Frances protested.

Petey ran in, wearing his nightshirt, his face rosy and scrubbed. "Come with me, Frankie," he said. "I'll show you where you'll sleep. It's in a room with me, but you have a bed all to yourself!"

Both Jake and Margaret looked chagrined. "We forgot to show you your room!" Margaret said. "With all the commotion, and the guests—oh, Frankie, I'm sorry."

"It's all right," Frances said, her mind still on the bath. She allowed herself to be led away by Petey.

The room where she and Petey would sleep was large enough for two beds and a small chest. Both beds had been layered with multicolored quilts, and the nightshirt the society had packed for Frances lay on one of the beds. There were a colorful rag rug on the wooden floor and cotton print curtains at the window, which overlooked the back of the house and the barn.

Frances stroked the top quilt, and Petey, his eyes shining with delight, whispered, "It's so soft!"

Frances grabbed the nightshirt and bolted down the stairs. "Please don't wait for me," she said to the Cummingses. "I'll take my bath and go right up to bed, soon as I bail the water out of the tub."

"Just throw the water out the back door onto the vegetable garden," Margaret said. "Soapy water drives away the bugs."

A steaming kettle was still hanging over the banked fire. Frances added it to the tub in which Petey had already taken his bath, quickly stripped off her clothes, and stepped in, scrunching down in the warm water with a sigh of delight. Finally she drained the tub a bucket at a time, mopped up the water she had spilled, went upstairs, and fell into bed, exhausted.

During the night Frances was awakened by the low murmur of voices, a door shutting, and the whinny of one of the horses.

She crept to the window, careful not to wake Petey. The moonlit yard was empty, the barn door shut. She waited silently, not moving, not breathing. The sounds did not return.

Frances quietly opened her bedroom door and slipped into the hall. The other bedroom door stood open, and in the dim light she could see that Margaret was asleep, but Jake's side of the bed was empty.

Someone is outside. Jake is with them. Who would arrive in the dark, as silent as the shadows, afraid to be seen or heard?

12

DURING THE NIGHT a fierce wind that Margaret called a norther blew down from Canada, icing the sky to a frosty blue. In the morning Frances bundled up in one of Jake's old coats. Margaret handed her a pair of woolen gloves and wrapped a scarf around her neck. "As soon as we can, we'll drive into town and get you boys some proper clothes," she said. "I should have thought of it while we were in St. Joe. It's been a long time since we lost—" For an instant Margaret's eyes looked at something only she could see, but she took a deep breath and said matter-of-factly, ". . . since we had children in the house."

Frances was so curious that she spoke without thinking. "You had children?"

"Yes," Margaret said. "Two boys. Eight years ago they died from diphtheria."

"I'm sorry," Frances murmured, miserable that she had intruded on Margaret's pain.

But Petey blurted out, "Is that why you took us? So you'd have children again?"

"Petey!" Frances scolded, but Margaret graciously smiled and nodded.

"Yes, and two finer boys couldn't be found anywhere. Now get along with you, Frankie. Petey, where are the mittens I gave you?"

Frances ran to the barn, the chill air stinging her cheeks. The barn was warm with heat from the animals and the pungent, earthy smells of their bodies and breath, hay, and droppings. She glanced into the shadows at the back of the barn, but there was no sign that anyone had been there.

Jake was already at work milking Dilly, the other cow, so Frances pulled off her gloves and set to milking Clover as though she had done it all her life, warming her cheek against Clover's body.

After the cows had been turned out and the pasture gate locked, Jake led Frances back to the barn and to a wall on which the horses' equipment hung. He pointed out and named the harness, bits, reins, and all that was needed to hitch the horses to the wagon.

"Think you can do it?" he asked.

"Yes," Frances said.

"Then let's give it a try."

"Now?" Frances gulped as she looked at the pair of tall, strong horses, and she stepped backward.

Jake laughed. "They're gentle enough, and they'll trust you once they get to know you." He entered the first stall, threw a bridle over Sal's head, and led her to Frances. "Here. Hang on with one hand and stroke her nose with the other. Just keep talking to her. She likes that."

The horses snorted air and stamped around a lot, but Frances kept her hands firm and her voice gentle.

"Hop up on the seat," Jake said, once the horses had been hitched to the wagon. "You'll be driving the wagon at times. Best you learn right now how to go about it."

Her hands trembling with excitement, Frances took the reins and repeated all Jake's instructions as they drove the horses and wagon down the road a short way and back to the barn.

Jake smiled at her. "You have an uncommonly gentle way with animals. They'll like working with you."

By the time the wagon was unhitched and the horses turned out to pasture, Frances was so proud of herself she couldn't stop grinning. And she couldn't wait to tell Petey about what she had done. Mike and Danny would love to hear about it, too. Maybe they were driving their own horses right now. She wished for a way to know at this very moment what they were doing.

When Margaret called them to the noon meal, she announced that Petey was in bed with a cough and a light fever. By suppertime Margaret had caught the fever herself. Her face was flushed as she steadied herself against the back of a kitchen chair.

"You go to bed," Frances told her. "I can do what needs to be done."

"There's a pot of beef and barley soup on the stove," Margaret told her. "It just needs stirring now and then. It should be ready soon. Taste it and see if it needs salt or maybe another onion or . . ."

Jake took Margaret's hand. "Get to bed," he said. "Frankie and I can take care of everything."

"There's plenty of soup. I made more than enough."
Margaret's glance flicked toward the barn.

"Fine," Jake said. "Now come with me."

As they left the kitchen, Frances pressed her nose
against the window that overlooked the barn. She couldn't
have missed Margaret's meaning. There *was* someone in
the barn! Someone she needed to feed in addition to her
family. Slaves on the route to freedom? Frances was
determined to find out.

As soon as she heard Margaret and Jake's bedroom
door close, Frances grabbed her coat from the hook
near the back door and ran toward the barn. She lifted
the bar that held the door closed for the night and
squeezed inside. Shadows were dark and long, but there
was still enough daylight for her to see. The cows turned
their big-eyed, curious stare on her, and the horses lifted
their heads, blowing through their nostrils and deliberately bumping the sides of their stalls.

Step by step, Frances walked to the back of the barn.
Someone had to be here. But where?

She climbed the ladder high enough so that she could
see across the hayloft. No one was there. Slowly she
climbed down, facing the back of the barn.

Frances looked around again. The loft extended at
least four feet beyond the first floor of the barn, but the
outside walls of the barn were straight and unbroken.
Then the realization hit her. There had to be a hidden
room beyond Daisy's stall. Jake had made it clear that
the Underground Railroad shouldn't concern her, but
she couldn't stop herself.

She ran her fingers up and down the boards, which
were firm until the pressure of her hands caused one to
give a little. Frances pushed again, but the board held
fast, as though someone were pressing even harder on

the other side. There was a knothole in the second board, and Frances stretched on tiptoe to look through it. She wasn't totally surprised to discover an eye looking back at her!

She stumbled back, letting out a yelp, as a hidden door in the wall swung inward. A black man stumbled out, and behind him stood a small, thin woman, whose shawl was wrapped closely around her back and shoulders.

"I know you're the slaves the bounty hunters are looking for," Frances whispered. "Don't be afraid of me! I want to help you!"

The man's broad shoulders seemed to droop with exhaustion. "We're trying to make our way north to Canada, and we were told we could find help at this place. Your pa said we could bed down here."

"This place is safe," she assured them. But the woman continued to look so frightened that Frances tried to put her at ease. "My name is Frankie," she said. "Who are you?"

The woman gave a little whimper and tugged at the man's sleeve. He shook his head. "We better hide again. Someone else might come."

"We'd hear the horses in plenty of time," Frances said. "Please talk to me."

They looked at each other a moment, then the man nodded. "I'm Janus. My wife is called Odette."

"Do you have any children?"

Odette nodded. "Our master took our son away from us when he was five years old and gave him as a wedding gift to his daughter, who was moving to a city far away." Her voice was dry, as though she had run out of tears to soften it.

"He gave away your son!" Frances was horrified.

"We begged, but it did no good," Odette said. "We knew we weren't never going to see our boy again. We wanted to take him and run, but he was gone before we knew about the Underground Railroad. Then four weeks ago, when we found out that Janus was going to be sold, we ran away."

"It's not fair!" Frances clenched her fists, furious at the man who had caused all their trouble. "Families shouldn't be torn apart!" She stopped abruptly as the picture of her own family flashed across her mind.

"I've brought some food." Jake's voice, behind Frances, startled her, and she whirled around. He stood just inside the door, holding a pot that smelled like Margaret's thick meat soup and a cloth-wrapped bundle that probably contained a loaf of bread. "This is my son Frankie," Jake told the couple. "He shouldn't have come out here, but we can trust him not to reveal anything." The glance that he turned on Frances was serious. "You told me that you wanted to help."

"I do," Frances said.

"Then get back to the house and take some soup to Margaret and Peter."

Without a word Frances turned and ran to the kitchen. By the time Jake returned, she had taken care of the invalids. She'd fed them and then, following Margaret's directions, she'd dipped strips of flannel in a mixture of gum camphor and goose oil and wrapped the cloths around Margaret's and Petey's throats to help stop their coughing. *Megan would have been much better at it,* Frances thought. All of Megan's shyness and unsureness disappeared when she comforted and nursed the younger children.

Frances fed Barker and quickly set places at the table for Jake and herself. Jake ate without speaking until his soup bowl was empty. Frances, afraid he was angry because she had gone to the barn, ate in silence as well. Finally Jake raised his head and asked, "Can you cook?"

"A little," Frances said, thinking of the limited foods her family had eaten. "I can make porridge."

"Fine. In the morning make plenty, and cook it thick so it will be filling. Is there enough bread?"

"Two more loaves, that's all. But I don't know how to bake bread."

Jake nodded. "I wouldn't expect a boy to. We'll make do." For the first time since they had met in the barn, he smiled at Frances.

He hadn't spoken yet about Odette and Janus, and Frances couldn't stand it any longer. "How long will they be here?" she blurted out.

Jake lowered his voice. "Until the time is right. Until we hear that the bounty hunters have moved on."

Frances wanted so much to help Odette and Janus. "I'd like to bring them the extra quilt on my bed," she told Jake.

"They have quilts enough," Jake said. "They're not the first to stay here in cold weather." He smiled. "But there will be plenty that you can do for them. I'll let you know when I need you."

"Oh, yes!" Frances said. "I'll do anything."

Jake leaned toward her. "Frankie, it would be dangerous for all of us if anyone learned about our part in the Underground Railroad. It's important that you not let on to *anyone* that you know that Janus and Odette are here. And you must never give away the hiding place."

"I promise!" Frances said. "No one will ever learn the secret from me!"

For the next two days, Frances not only tended to

144

the household chores and to Margaret and Petey, but at times carried meals to Janus and Odette. She'd stay to talk with them, and they began to relax and talk to her.

"When will they go?" she asked Jake.

"As soon as it's safe, someone will let me know."

Frances was delighted when Petey grew too energetic to keep in bed and when Margaret, still a little weak, rose even before Frances to bake bread. The brick oven warmed the kitchen, and the sweet, yeasty fragrance of the rising loaves filled the room.

That morning Frances carried in the pails of milk alone because Jake had picked up a cough so strong that it shook his body. She found Margaret sitting in the wide Boston rocker, snuggling Petey in her lap. Frances, so tired of pretending to be a boy, yearned to be able to curl up on Margaret's lap, too.

Petey beamed at Frances. "Mama sang me three songs! And she's going to teach me one about a pony to ride."

Mama? Frances took a sudden breath. The word was a blow that stunned and confused her. This was what she had wanted, wasn't it? For Petey to have someone to love him and snuggle him and care for him, in place of the mother who heartlessly sent him away?

Margaret reached for Frances's hand. "Thank you for your wonderful care," she said. "There is so much tenderness in you, Frankie. You cared for us as well as any woman could."

Now is the time to tell the truth, Frances thought. *I can't stand to go on pretending to be a boy much longer. Petey is happy and he has another mother to love him, even if they send me away.* "There's something I must explain to you," she began to tell Margaret.

At that moment Jake stumbled into the house, banging the door behind him. His face was flushed, and he dropped into the nearest chair, shaking and coughing.

Margaret put Petey down and jumped up. "You have the fever, Jake. Come. You need to rest in bed."

Jake shook his head. "The signs are that the weather will close in soon. I must take Janus and Odette to Klaus Mueller's today."

"You can't," Margaret said stubbornly. "You're in no condition to go!"

"They can't stay here. Once the winter storms come, they won't be able to make it to Canada."

"We'll—we'll find someone else who can take them. Maybe Carl Busby."

"Carl is not a part of the railroad."

"But in this case—"

"We can't take the chance."

Frances was terrified, but Jake needed the help she had promised, and so did Odette and Janus. She had no other choice. She tried to sound brave and determined. "Let me go," she said. "I can do it."

"It's too much for you to handle," Jake said. "There's a full load of corn fodder to take, too."

Frances was insistent. "Janus can help me load the sacks on the wagon inside the barn. You know I can take care of the rest. And I can keep the secret."

Margaret looked at Frances, then at her husband. "It's only half a day's drive to the Muellers' farm. If Frankie follows the road north, he can't get lost." She turned to Frances. "All you have to do is follow the road. It will take you over the border into Nebraska Territory. The river will be low enough to ford easily. The Muellers' farm will be the first one you come to."

Jake tried to speak, but he shook with another spasm of coughing.

Margaret was firm. "Let him do it, Jake. You're so ill that the drive could kill you! I'm sure those bounty hunters must have left this area days ago."

Before Jake could answer, Margaret began to pack food for Frances, Janus, and Odette. Frances bundled up and hurried to the barn.

"It's time to leave," she told Janus and Odette, hoping they weren't able to see the way her hands trembled. "We'll make a hiding place for you among the sacks. No one will suspect that you're traveling in broad daylight."

"Where's your pa?" Janus stared at her with concern.

"He's too ill to go," she said. "I'm going to take you."

"You're just a child."

Frances shook her head. "That's all to the good, I'm thinking. Who would suspect a—a boy? I'll need you to help me load the sacks. We'll have to hurry."

They worked together quickly, loading the sacks, leaving a trench down the middle where Janus and Odette could lie. They harnessed the horses and laid a canvas sheet over the wagon. When Frances was satisfied that Janus and Odette were as comfortable as possible, she tied down the canvas at the wagon's four corners.

Margaret brought the food to the wagon—two parcels, one for Frances, one for Janus and Odette. "Be very, very careful." Margaret hugged Frances tightly. "Stay on the road," she added, "and watch for any sudden changes in the weather."

Frances smiled. "I'll get them there all right." She hugged Margaret tightly. She realized how much she cared for Margaret and Jake, who were becoming like family to her. They were good people and kind, and she wouldn't let them down.

She hopped up on the seat, clucked to the horses, and drove the wagon onto the road, heading north.

147

Frances saw no one else on the road. It was a gray day, with a buildup of clouds to the north, and the wind stung her face. At first Frances was nervous and glanced often from side to side, but as the miles went by she began to relax. She wished Mike and Danny were with her. Wouldn't she love to show Mike how well she could handle a team of horses! He'd probably never let on he was proud of her, but he would be, and Danny would beg to be allowed to handle the reins.

She ate the bread and meat that Margaret had prepared for her and looked out across the low rolling hills, where the grasses shivered in waves and ripples. To the east she caught glimpses now and then of a narrow band of silvery water that twisted through the stands of cottonwoods, aspens, and maples. The river began to curve to the west, and Frances knew she was getting close to the place where they could ford it.

With one gloved hand Frances rubbed the back of her neck, arching her shoulders and stretching. Jake and Margaret had no reason to be concerned for her. She had brought the wagon almost to Nebraska, and nothing had happened.

Suddenly, from behind them, came shouts and hoofbeats. Frances knew she had relaxed too soon. Terrified, she looked over her shoulder and saw the marshal and the two bounty hunters racing toward her.

13

FRANCES PULLED THE horses to a halt, cringing as one bounty hunter stopped so close to her that she could see the red veins in his windburned eyes.

"Jake's new boy. Frankie, isn't it?" Marshal Dawson asked, then, giving her no time to answer, he added, "Where are you off to?"

"I—I'm taking a load of corn to Mr. Mueller's farm," she stammered, "because Jake can't do it. He's ill with the fever." She tried not to meet his eyes and prayed that the secret she carried didn't show on her face.

"Sorry to hear that Jake's ailing," the marshal said.

One of the bounty hunters interrupted him. "Since the boy's goin' into Nebraska, he may have more than corn in that load."

"That could be so," the other bounty hunter said. He leaned close to peer into her face. Frances shot him a look of hatred and anger and quickly turned away. She tried to keep her hands from shaking by gripping the reins tightly and pressing them against her knees.

Frances's stomach clutched, and she held her breath as one of the bounty hunters slowly rode to the back of the wagon to poke at the canvas and the sacks of corn with the barrel end of his rifle.

"You seen any sign of those runaways?" the other bounty hunter asked. "Remember—a man and a woman. And she's got an embroidered shawl. Stole it from her mistress."

Frances remembered how Mike had taught her to face the street bullies in New York. These men seemed no different, so a show of spunk would be her best defense. She knew they were watching her closely for any sign of fear, which would let them know their suspicions had been right, so with all her might she fought her terror, stared scornfully, and retorted, "Stole it? That's not the truth. The marshal said that the woman *gave* it to her."

"You got a good memory," he said. "So remember this. Anyone who helps slaves escape can get sent to prison."

"He's just a boy doin' a job for his pa," the marshal said. "Let him get on his way. It's going to snow soon."

The men guided their horses back a few steps, then whirled and rode in the direction from which they had come.

Frances's hands shook inside her heavy gloves, and it was hard to hold the reins, but just in case they had glanced back to watch her, she sat straight as a new board and clucked to the horses to start up again.

It wasn't until they were out of sight that Frances finally was able to breathe normally. The wagon rolled on. At last the narrow river crossed their path ahead, and she soothed the horses down the bank and into the shallow water. She could easily see farm buildings on the other side. The Muellers' farm. She was weak with relief when she finally drove into the yard and up to the barn.

Mr. Mueller ran out to meet her, grasping the horses' bridles and leading them into the barn. "You get into the house," he said. "I'll take care of everything."

As Frances entered the warm kitchen, Johnny grinned at her.

"My pa never let *me* drive the wagon alone," he said.

Frances clutched Mrs. Mueller's arm with fingers still stiff from the cold and whispered, "The bounty hunters stopped me. They're still looking for a woman wearing that embroidered shawl. This time they said she stole it. Odette mustn't wear it any longer. She can take my coat."

"You need your own coat," Mrs. Mueller said in hushed tones. "We have extras, and we'll give one to her." Her voice returned to normal. "Now, Frankie, don't waste time with worry. Use your energies to eat." She propelled Frances to the table and put a plate of hot potatoes, carrots, and boiled beef in front of her.

While his brothers concentrated on their meals, Johnny leaned across the table and whispered, "Tell me about the slaves. How many were there?"

"Two," Frances mumbled, her mouth full.

"Let Frankie eat his food in peace," Mrs. Mueller said, frowning at Johnny as she tossed quick glances at his younger brothers. "This is not the time for talk."

Later, after the younger three boys had been sent to bed, Johnny told Frances, "You brought them by yourself. You're really brave!"

"I wasn't brave. I was frightened," Frances confided.

He shook his head. "That doesn't matter. You were brave enough to take a big chance and break the law! If you were caught, you'd go to prison!"

"Johnny!" Mrs. Mueller warned.

"I didn't want to break the law," Frances said, "and it didn't seem wrong to help those people."

"It wasn't wrong," Mrs. Mueller said.

Frances slowly shook her head. "It's such a muddle. The people who obey the laws, like those bounty hunters, are really doing the wrong thing; and the people who try to help the slaves reach freedom are right, but they're breaking the laws!"

Mr. Mueller had slipped into the kitchen in time to hear most of the discussion. He nodded from his seat by the fire. "In this case, at least, you did not do a bad thing, Frankie. The people who help slaves to find freedom have chosen to take the risk of going to prison, to make a sacrifice to help someone else."

"Sacrifice," Frances said, repeating the word she had heard her mother use. She sighed. "I've heard adults talk of sacrifice, but I don't really understand all that it means."

Mrs. Mueller pulled off her apron and hung it on a hook on the side of a cupboard. "Sacrifice is not always easy to understand, Frankie. It means that someone or something else means more to you than your own self. Let me explain it this way—it means that you can love someone or some idea enough to give up something that you prize, in order to make people's lives better. You understand that, Frankie. Today, to help others, you made a sacrifice."

She patted Frances's shoulder. "Enough talk," she said. "It's time for this boy to get his rest." She led Frances to a bed in the room with the little boys, who were bundled into quilts on the floor. "Sleep," she said. "You're so tired that your eyes will close the moment you pull the quilt around your ears. We want you to have a good night's rest, because if the weather is clear tomorrow you will have that long ride back."

Frances's eyes did not close right away. She kept repeating to herself Mrs. Mueller's explanation of sacrifice. If you love someone enough to give up something you prize—*Is this what you were trying to tell me, Ma, when I was too angry and hurt to really listen?*

Ma's face, as it had looked in the courthouse hallway, appeared before her. Frances could see the pain in her mother's eyes as she remembered her words: "Help me, love. Help me to make them understand."

A hard knot inside Frances's chest melted with such a rush of tears that she curled tightly underneath the quilt to smother the sound, whispering again and again, "Oh, Ma! Ma, I *do* understand!"

Morning broke clear, the night's snowfall leaving only a fine dusting of white across the hills. Frances quickly pulled on her clothes and hurried downstairs.

"How are Janus and Odette?" Frances asked as she devoured a huge breakfast of eggs, biscuits, and frizzled ham slices.

"They're fine," Mrs. Mueller said. "They've been given warm clothing and food and sent on their way long ago. No one will be able to stop them now. I can promise you that."

Frances leaned back in her chair with a happy sigh. She had done it! She had helped them to escape! She could hardly wait to get home to tell Jake and Margaret. "I should leave, too," she told Mrs. Mueller. "I'm needed at home, because Jake is too ill to do the chores."

Johnny dashed into the room. "I heard what Frankie said, and I've got a good plan. I'll ride home with him and help. I'll even take a turn with the horses."

"Sure, that's a grand idea!" Frances exclaimed.

"Just how would you get home, Johnny?"

"Uh—Frankie could drive me back."

"And once more back and forth?" Mrs. Mueller laughed. "Frankie is capable of driving alone. He's proved what he can do."

"Awww," Johnny complained. "Pa never lets me drive alone, and I'm a year older than Frankie."

His mother gave him a playful swat on his bottom. "Since you are so old you must be very strong, so you can go out and help hitch Frankie's wagon. Get along with you!"

Along with food for the journey, Mrs. Mueller carried to the barn a length of dress fabric, a seedcake, and a pot of cheese to take to Margaret. "We'll find something with which to wrap that cheese well, so the cold won't spoil it."

Frances, eager to get on her way, spotted the black shawl and picked it up. "I can use this," she said. She wrapped the cheese and tucked the packages into a corner of the wagon. Then she folded the canvas next to them.

"Take care," Mrs. Mueller told her, and Johnny yelled, "I'll see you at the Christmas party!"

Frances waved and led the horses south on the road toward home.

Although icy, the river was still easy to ford. The horses stepped briskly as though they knew they were headed for home. With no load to take back, the nearly empty wagon bounced on the road, and the team, with less to pull, made better time. Frances hummed to herself, delighted at the picture in her mind of Janus and Odette reaching freedom in Canada. As soon as all the slaves had been freed and she didn't need to keep the Underground Railroad secret any longer, she would write to Mike and tell him all about the adventure—and Ma, too. Wouldn't Mike think it a grand thing and wish he'd been with her! And she could almost hear Ma saying, "Ah, love, it's so very proud of you I am."

She'd write the story to Megan, too. As the two eldest girls in the family, she and Megan had always shared a special bond. When Megan heard about Odette and Janus's freedom, she'd be just as happy for them as Frances was now.

Although the white-frosted hills were serene under a clear sky, the wind prickled Frances's face with sharp slivers of cold, so she kept urging Sal and Daisy to keep up their pace. As she looked west she thought long about Megan. The couple who took her had a home out on that prairie. It was so far away, and Frances missed her sister so much. She hoped the isolated prairie life would not be hard on the gentle, sensitive Megan.

Frances missed Ma, too. She could hardly wait to get to the Cummingses' farm so she could write to her mother. When she wrote to tell Ma of her adventure, Frances would also tell her that she'd been wrong—that now she really did understand Ma's sacrifice.

Frances was almost home when the marshal and the two bounty hunters suddenly appeared on the road. They'd never know how close they'd come to the slaves they'd been tracking. They'd ride on, retracing their steps toward the north, searching for Odette and Janus in vain. Frances raised a hand to wave at the marshal and was surprised when he turned with the bounty hunters and rode beside her for a few moments.

"Glad the weather didn't close in on you," he said.

"It was an easy trip," Frances answered. She was aware that one of the men was poking the barrel of his rifle in the back of the wagon. She suppressed a smile. He wasn't going to find any hidden slaves behind the cake and cheese.

The cheese! Suddenly Frances realized that she foolishly had used Odette's shawl to wrap the pot of cheese! How could she have been so stupid? She froze, clinging to the reins so tightly her fingers became numb.

"Give my regards to your folks," Marshal Dawson said, and he urged his horse on. But one of the bounty hunters suddenly yelled, "Wait a minute, Marshal! Pull up, boy!" He pointed his rifle at her head to make sure that she obeyed.

The man grabbed the wrapped pot of cheese and shook the shawl until its contents tumbled into the wagon. He waved the shawl over his head. "Ain't this what that slave woman was wearin'?"

The other bounty hunter examined it closely. "Looks like."

"Where did you get this shawl?" the marshal asked Frances, and this time his voice was stern.

"I found it on the ground," Frances said truthfully. "I used it to wrap the cheese so it wouldn't freeze."

"On the ground where?" Marshal Dawson asked.

Frances lifted her chin, staring back. No matter how frightened she was, she wasn't about to give him an answer.

"We can figure that out," one bounty hunter said to his partner. "C'mon, let's head north. You take care of this lawbreakin' boy, Marshal."

He tossed the shawl into the wagon, and the two of them set off at a gallop.

Janus and Odette had been given a long head start. Mrs. Mueller had promised that they'd be in no more danger, and the Muellers could handle these two ruffians, so Frances didn't worry about them. She only wanted to get home to Jake and Margaret. Could they help her? What would become of her?

"I'll ride back with you to Jake's place." The marshal's words broke into her thoughts. "'You know, son, that as of now you're under arrest."

Frances jumped as though he'd struck her. Under arrest! Did that mean she'd go to prison? She shuddered. Would Jake and Margaret be arrested, too? What would happen to Petey? Her new parents had made a home for her, and now everything was about to be lost. Tears spilled from her eyes, stinging her cheeks. She'd lose her new family and her old family!

It was true she had broken the law. There was no question about it, so she'd have to accept the punishment. She couldn't be saved the way Mike had been saved. There was nowhere left to send her. *It's all so unfair!* she thought. *If a law hurts people, then shouldn't it be broken?* Frances concentrated on driving the wagon, angrily rubbing away the tears.

As they reached the house, Marshal Dawson was firm with Jake, who had come out on the porch. The marshal explained what had been found in the wagon and what it obviously meant.

"Frankie is innocent of breaking any law," Jake said. "He's a child. Any fault that may be found is mine."

"Frankly," the marshal said, "my sympathies lie with the abolitionists, but I'm sworn to uphold the law. I've got no proof that you had anything to do with this, Jake, so I'm not puttin' you under arrest, but whether you had or not, I've still got to arrest this boy and take him to town to be charged."

"That shawl is your only proof!" Margaret objected. "Frankie said he found it! Anyone could have dropped it!"

Petey ran out on the porch calling, "They're coming! They're coming! I saw them from the window upstairs!"

Everyone turned to look in the direction Petey was pointing. "See!" Petey yelled. "Mr. MacNair and Mrs. Banks said they'd come and see us, and there they are!"

"Oh, no!" Frances whispered, in agony that they should see her being arrested. "Not now!"

The marshal put a firm hand on Frances's shoulder. "I have to take the boy with me," he said.

Margaret pushed his hand away. "No!" she cried. "Frankie is my son, and I won't let you have him!"

Jake, even more pale than before, stepped between Frances and the marshal. "We need to talk, Marshal Dawson. But let's wait until Andrew MacNair gets here. Frankie is still under Andrew's supervision."

Andrew tied their horses to the rail as Katherine ran up onto the porch. She put her arms on Margaret's shoulders and studied her face. "What's wrong?" she asked. "What happened?"

"I'll tell you," the marshal said, and proceeded to list the facts.

Katherine shook her head and laughed, while Margaret gasped and said, "Katherine! This situation is not humorous!"

"Of course it is," Katherine said. "It's nonsense." She smiled at the marshal. "Do you actually believe that a little thirteen-year-old girl could do all that you say?"

"Girl?"

Everyone turned and stared at Frances, who began to

blush furiously. "I—I'm sorry," she stammered. "It's true. I really am a girl. I didn't know what to do except pose as a boy. I overheard Mr. MacNair say that boys were easier to place together, and I'd promised our ma that I'd take care of Petey. I borrowed Mike's knife to cut my hair and put on some boys' clothes." She looked around the group, from face to face. Jake's mouth fell open, Margaret's eyebrows shot up, and Andrew looked completely bewildered. "It did work out," Frances added, "because Petey and I were able to stay together!"

The marshal cleared his throat a couple of times before he said, "I can't just take your word for it, young man—uh, well—whoever you are. I suppose I'll need proof."

Frances shrank back against Margaret, who shouted at the marshal, "Oh, no you won't!"

For a moment he looked bewildered, then his face turned a dark red. "Well, I—I didn't mean—" he stuttered.

Katherine smiled at the marshal. "As I see it, we have only one problem to settle—the ownership of that shawl. You said it was a black shawl, with blue embroidered flowers in the corner?"

He nodded.

"Why, Marshal Dawson," she said, "I do believe that could be mine. If you're ever in St. Joe, I'll see if I can find a bill of sale for it."

Marshal Dawson pursed his lips together and rubbed hard at his chin. Frances wondered if he were trying to keep from laughing. "It appears there's been a big mistake here," he said, and a broad smile succeeded in escaping. "We now have no evidence that a crime has been committed, and, in any case, there's no way I'm going to arrest a little girl."

Touching the brim of his hat and nodding to the

women, this time including Frances, he got back on his horse and rode away.

For a moment no one spoke. It was more than Frances could take. "It's so very tired I am of pretending to be a boy!" she cried. "Even if you send me away, I need to be myself! I need to be a girl again! I didn't want to lie to you, and I can't do it anymore!" Her tears burst out in a torrent.

Margaret's arms were around her, hugging her, holding her, stroking back her cropped hair. And it was Margaret's voice she heard soothing her, saying, "Oh, Frankie, I love having a daughter!"

Frances held Margaret tightly, the love she felt melting away all the mixed-up feelings that had been tormenting her. She would always love Ma, whether she could be with her or not, but she had a new home with people who loved her, too, who generously shared their life with Petey and her. What an enormous relief it was, not having to pretend any longer to be someone she wasn't!

It occurred to her with a jolt that there was something she'd forgotten, and maybe Margaret and Jake had, too. She pulled away from Margaret, turning earnestly to Jake. "Because I'm a girl it doesn't mean I can't still help you with the farm work. I'm strong and I work hard. You saw how quickly I learned to milk the cows and handle the horses. I—"

Jake lifted a hand to quiet Frances. For a moment he seemed to think about it. Then he grinned, and Frances knew he'd been pretending. "I'd just as soon work with a daughter as with a son," he said. His eyes became serious. "No son could make me any more proud than I am right now of you, Frankie."

"Not *Frankie*! Her name is really Frances Mary!"

160

Petey shouted in a rush. "It's not a secret anymore, so I can tell her real name!" He broke off, clapping a hand over his mouth, and whispered cautiously, "Can't I?"

Laughing, the men led the horses off to the barn to care for them, Petey on their heels.

Frances took the handkerchief Margaret handed her and wiped her eyes, staring with wonder at Katherine. "How did you know I was a girl?"

"Two reasons." Katherine reached into the cloth purse that hung at her waist and pulled out a letter. "Your mother wrote to ask about the welfare of her children, telling something about each of you and giving your full names." She handed the envelope to Frances. "I know you'd like to read her letter."

"Oh, yes!" Frances said, clutching it eagerly.

Katherine continued. "Finding you were a Frances Mary instead of a Frankie didn't come as that much of a surprise to me." She lowered her voice and grinned at Frances. "I began to suspect that you were a girl by the way you looked at Andrew MacNair."

Frances felt her cheeks grow warm, and she ducked her head.

"He's too old for you," Katherine teased.

"But not for *you*," Margaret added with a chuckle. "However, that's just between us women."

Frances laughed, hugging Margaret again. "Wait until my brothers and sisters find out what has happened!" she exclaimed.

"Mike will think it's more exciting than a dime novel," Katherine said.

"As far as I'm concerned," Frances said, "the best thing is that now I'm back to being a girl!"

Grandma Briley gently closed the cover of the journal and lightly patted the soft blue binding.

Jennifer leaned forward eagerly. "Don't stop!"

"Yeah!" Jeff said. "Tell us more!"

Grandma got out of her chair and pinched two shriveled leaves from a hanging basket of pothos ivy. "Not now," she said. "I'm going to make dinner early, because the City Council is meeting tonight. But if you'd like me to, I'll tell you Mike's story tomorrow."

"What about those people who adopted Mike?" Jeff asked.

"I didn't like them," Jennifer said.

"Neither did Mike," Grandma told her.

"I suspected them right away," Jeff said.

Grandma looked mysterious. "Then you won't be surprised to find out that Mike was suspicious of them, too. Why, Mike even began to wonder if Mr. Friedrich had committed a murder!"

"Murder?" Mike said. "Tell us—did he?"

"For now you can help me set the table," Grandma teased. "Mike's story will just have to wait until tomorrow."

ABOUT THE AUTHOR

JOAN LOWERY NIXON is the acclaimed author of more than eighty books for children and young adults. She is a three-time winner of the Mystery Writers of America Edgar Award and the recipient of many Children's Choice Awards. Popular books for young adults include *A Family Apart*, *Caught in the Act*, and *A Place to Belong*, the other books in the Orphan Train Quartet for which she received two Golden Spur Awards, the Hollywood Daughters trilogy, as well as *High Trail to Danger* and its companion novel, *A Deadly Promise*. Mrs. Nixon is currently working on her new Ellis Island novels.

Mrs. Nixon and her husband live in Houston, Texas.

STARFIRE

Books *you'll* want
to read...and keep

☐ HOME SWEET HOME
by Jeanne Betancourt
16-year-old Tracy Jensen is not looking forward to leaving New York City to move with her family to her grandmother's farm. Tracy feels isolated at first, but when she meets Russian exchange student Anya and gets involved in the town's activities she sees that life on the land offers many more rewards than she'd ever anticipated. 27857-6 $2.95/$3.50 in Canada

☐ THE SILVER GLOVE
by Suzie McKee Charnas
Heroine of *The Bronze King*, 14-year-old Valentine Marsh must help her remarkable, magical grandmother fight a powerful wizard who's come to Earth to steal human souls—and is masquerading as Val's new school psychologist! *The Silver Glove* is full of suspense, chilling chase scenes, magic & love.
27853-3 $2.95/$3.50 in Canada

☐ CAUGHT IN THE ACT: ORPHAN TRAIN QUARTET, BOOK 2 by Joan Lowery Nixon
In the second novel of THE ORPHAN TRAIN QUARTET, 11-year-old, Mike fears that he will be sent back to New York City to serve his prison sentence as a convicted thief. But the German family which has adopted him seems to be involved in much worse than stealing—murder! Mike vows to uncover the truth, even if his own life is in danger.
27912-2 $2.95/$3.50 in Canada

☐ THE GIRL WHO INVENTED ROMANCE
by Caroline B. Cooney, author of 'Among Friends'
As she watches her friends and family playing at romance, 16-year-old Kelly Williams has a great idea—she'll create a board game that sets down the rules of the romance game. It's easy for Kelly to see how others should act, but it's much more difficult when it comes to her own feelings for Will! (A Starfire Hardcover).
05473-2 $13.95/$15.95 in Canada